No Way

Am I Living With Her!

Caroline Plaisted worked in publishing
for fourteen years, latterly as editorial manager for
BBC Books, before writing her own books.
She has had more than forty books published,
including *E-Love, Reality Bites Back!, Re-inventing
Mum* and *Living with a Re-invented Mum*. She lives in
Kent with her two children, two dogs and two cats.

No Way

Am I Living With Her!

Caroline Plaisted

Piccadilly Press • London

First published in Great Britain in 2004
by Piccadilly Press Ltd.,
5 Castle Road, London NW1 8PR
www.piccadillypress.co.uk

A catalogue record for this book is available from the
British Library

ISBN: 1 85340 840 9 (trade paperback)

1 3 5 7 9 8 6 4 2

Printed and bound in Great Britain by Bookmarque Ltd
Text design by Textype
Cover illustration by Sue Hellard
Cover design by Fielding Design
Set in Bembo and Tempus

Chapter **One**

It's a well-known fact that parents were invented simply so that they can embarrass their children. Picture it:

Mums are around so that they can criticise your clothes and lay into you when you are late back. They prefer to do this in front of your friends to make sure they really rub it in. Oh – and they are also extremely good at saying something that's just so cringe-making to your teachers. Like when they suddenly decide that you once said you wanted to be a research chemist when you were about seven and then a zillion years later they go and blab about it to your chemistry teacher at parents' evening. Nice one, Mum. Now Mr Bunsen Burner keeps giving me these totally dull magazines about test tubes and then asking me about them at the next lesson . . . Der-er!

Then there's dads, who are there so that they can scrutinise all your friends – male and female – and make comments about them. 'Are you sure her brother isn't a drug dealer? I mean, he's got a bolt through his eyebrow!' (That's what my friend Helen said her dad actually said about our other friend Jemma and her brother. Honest!) And Ru (he's my cousin) says that dads go on about clothes just as much as mums. He said my Uncle Joe said once: 'Why can't you wear trousers that actually fit you? I can see your boxers for goodness' sake!' Ru also says that my uncle nags about homework, where he's been – the works, really. So dads are just as bad as mums.

But personally, I don't have that much experience of dads. The last time I saw my dad was five years ago, when I was eight. He went out one day and never came back. I remember it like it was yesterday, not five years ago. I was in my summer uniform (red gingham dress with a white collar – bless!), sitting at the table eating my Rice Krispies. Dad gave me a kiss on my head and said, 'See you later, sunshine!' Then he kissed my mum and said, 'And you!' Then he went off to the station in his car. And that was the last time I saw him.

Problem was, he didn't get to the station because he swerved to avoid a little boy who ran out into the road chasing his ball and drove straight into the side of a lorry and was killed. Just like that. One minute I had a dad. The next I didn't.

When I was first told, it didn't really sink in – didn't seem real. After a while, though, I realised that Dad really wasn't going to come back any more. Not ever. Of course, I cried my eyes out. But then I got angry, really angry. With Dad. I mean, how dare my mum and I be left alone like that! It was all right for Dad, though, wasn't it? The coroner said that he wouldn't have known anything because he was killed instantly. He never suffered, he said.

He might not have suffered but Mum and I did. I may have only been eight, but I was old enough to realise that Mum had loads of stuff to sort out. I remember there being loads of forms for her to fill in – I've no idea what they were all about, though. And she was always having to go to see people and leaving me to play with Ru at Auntie Liz's. I shouldn't think that you've ever really thought about your husband's funeral when you are only in your thirties – who would? But my mum had to. Up till then, Mum (she's a primary school teacher) had worked part-time but after the accident she started working full-time. Instead of my mum coming to collect me almost every day after school, now I always had to go home with Auntie Liz.

Mum cried a lot, too. And I felt bad because I couldn't do anything to stop her or make her feel better. But at least Mum still had the school holidays to be with me, so that was almost like it had been before. Almost. It took me a while to get used to it always being Mum, or just Mum and no Dad, taking me to the cinema, or going down to the beach when we were on holiday.

And one of the worst things was the way other people 'coped' with it. I suppose people felt sorry for us – and most of them acted like real muppets. Some people just ignored us. Literally. We'd be standing at the bus stop and some woman we'd known for ever would come up to the bus stop, start acting like she'd suddenly seen a really interesting poster in the bus shelter, start staring at it – and say nothing. Then she'd leap on to the bus when it arrived and disappear upstairs.

But then the other people who did speak to us about it would usually say too much. 'I don't know how you cope' was a typical comment they'd make to my mum. And I'd want to scream at them, 'Because we don't have any choice, you stupid person!' Only I never did. I just smiled and said thank you and Mum and I gave each other a look. The look that meant we both knew how we felt but no one else could even begin to understand and, whatever anyone said, it wasn't going to change what had happened. There were other people who

4

would keep giving me money – I remember I got lots of pound coins. What did they think I was going to do with the money? Buy another dad? The first couple of times it was OK. I just spent the money on sweets. But I soon realised that the money was a substitute for people not being able to say 'I think what's happened to you and your mum is the pits' and I began to think that adults were pretty useless.

But don't get me wrong. After a while everything settled down. I still missed Dad – but I kind of got used to missing him, and me and Mum were OK. I've got my own way of handling the missing-my-dad bit, though. I suppose if some people knew about it, they might think I was a bit crazy but it works for me. It was my teacher who got me started just after the accident. She knew how angry I was with Dad for leaving us. So she suggested that I wrote a letter to him telling him how I felt. I thought she was bonkers at first – even to an eight year old it seemed nuts to write a letter to someone who couldn't even read it. But then one night I couldn't sleep. I was lying in bed with all this stuff going round and round in my mind. I was cross and crying at the same time. And I just couldn't go and tell my mum. Even then I knew that she had enough of her own problems to cope with. And that made me angry, too! I wanted someone to come and take all my hurting bits away and put my dad back in his car, driving a different route to the station that morning.

So I lay in my bed that night, tossing and turning. What did my teacher really know about what was going on inside my head? So I thought I'd show her how stupid her idea was! I grabbed a notebook and found a pencil and started writing. But I had so much to yell at Dad about that I couldn't stop. I wrote and wrote in my scruffy and slow little eight-year-old handwriting.

At the time it didn't really make me less angry – not right away. And, of course, it didn't really change anything, either. But – if this doesn't make me seem like a saddo – I actually like writing. I'm one of those creeps at school who feels pleased when the teacher gives you creative writing to do. In fact, I want to be a writer – maybe a journalist – when I leave school.

Anyway, I've never stopped writing letters to Dad, telling him about what's going on and how I feel. Wondering about what he'd do about stuff if he was still around. And it helps – it took me a long while. Five years, I suppose. You see, once you've got the words down on paper it kind of gets them out of your head and frees up the space for other stuff. There was only space for a little bit of good stuff at first. But as time went on, I began to have space for more of it – and less space for the rotten stuff.

Now I write my dad a letter most weeks. I tell him when I'm upset, or when I've done well in a race (I'm into athletics as well as writing), most stuff. Of course, there's no address to post the letters to. So I keep them in a box, under my bed, at the moment. If my mum knows the box is there, she's never mentioned it. But I try to swap hiding places so that she doesn't find it. And as the years have gone by, I've had to get a couple more boxes and put letters in them, too. Like I said, I've got used to missing my dad and it's OK now. Well, sort of. I mean, there are kids at school who don't live with their dads because they're divorced and stuff. But at least they still get to see their dads. Death is different – it's for always. And for me it's become normal.

In our new version of normal life (like what, I now realise, is normal?), my mum would have a boyfriend every now and then. He'd take us out to places, and it would be cool. Mum still teaches at the same school – she has the really tiny ones who start in Reception and she's brilliant at it. You can tell she really loves her job because she's always sitting in the kitchen surrounded by bits of paper, yoghurt pots and glue, getting some project ready for school the next day. And there's always a big plastic crate with books and stuff in the hallway – stuff that she's brought home with her to mark or do things with.

In fact, the only criticism I've got about Mum is that she's a bit too relaxed about the yoghurt pots being everywhere. Ru (he's my cousin, remember?) says I'm really lucky because most other kids are getting it in the neck all the time about tidying up and not making a mess. In our house it's more likely to be me that moans about it! I just like a bit of order in life – it makes me feel in control. But don't get me wrong – I don't think that housework is fun or anything weird like that! How sad would that be?

Now like I said, Mum has boyfriends every now and then. But the boyfriend she's got at the moment has been around for a year or so. He's called Peter and he's mostly OK. He's a solicitor and he hangs around some nights in the week and stays some weekends. He even came to cheer me on when I ran in a race the other day. At the beginning of the year, though, things changed with Peter and Mum. Mum told me that she and Peter are going to get married. So that meant that Peter was going to be my stepdad.

'Isn't it great?' Mum said. 'Peter's daughters are going to be your sisters!'

Dear Dad,

Mum is downstairs in the kitchen going through another one of those wedding magazines. They are so boring. I asked her why she needed to look at yet another one. I mean, she's been looking through wedding books, catalogues and magazines since January! Mum says she has to keep looking just in case she sees some new idea that she hasn't thought of! I'm so fed up with all this wedding rubbish that I'm almost looking forward to the wedding so that we can get it over with.

Then I'll have two princesses for stepsisters. Aaagh! Honestly, Dad, I wish you could meet them. They are just so precious! And fancy having such stupid names! Africa and India! How daft are they? Imagine it, Dad! If you and Mum had called me after one of your holidays I would be called Camber or Suffolk! Stop the world – I want to jump off!

I've met Affie and Indie (I know – but slightly easier to say than their full names, eh?) a few times now but it doesn't get any

9

better. Being with them, I mean. Indie is slightly better. She's the older one. She's dead pretty, I'll say that for her. And dead tall. She's got great clothes, too. She's at university – maybe that's why she's a bit more relaxed about life than Affie. Affie is just too much. Too too much. She's tall, as well. But she is just so stuck up! She looks like she's got a bad smell under her nose all the time. Like by smiling, she'll somehow join this really scary place called the human race.

Peter (don't worry, Dad, I still have no intention of ever calling him 'dad') never tells Affie off either. Sometimes she is so rude! To him, to Mum – anyone. She answers back in this really sarcastic way. It is so not fair! If I spoke to Mum like that or Peter even – Mum would be totally stressy! I would never get away with it. But Affie does – every time! And she makes out she goes to this really superior school, too. Ooo-er, Affie!

Auntie Liz doesn't like her – I know she doesn't. She's only seen her once, but I could tell. And every time she mentions her name, she curls her top lip as if she's about to gag on it. Auntie Liz is a bit weird, too, at the moment. She used to really like Peter before. But now she's kind of strange with him. You know – kind of off with him. It's only been since he and Mum told everyone they were getting married, though. What is it with you grown-ups, Dad? Why do you all act like kids all the time?

But even Ru's gone a bit odd. We used to go out running during the week – a couple of nights at least, round the track in the park. But now when I ask him he says he's busy – or he kind of grunts it, anyway. Only he isn't busy because it's not like he's ever doing anything. All he does is lie around in his room watching telly. Or lie around in the living room at Auntie Liz's watching telly. When he's not doing that, he's with his mate Marco. And when he's with Marco, Ru won't speak to me at all! What have I done to upset him? It's not my fault he's started to get zits on his chin. (They are really pus-y ones, too - yuck!)

At least Cath isn't all strange with me. She

says she's going to come along as my cheerleader at my next race, Dad! It's in a couple of weeks' time – an inter-school athletics thing. I think that girl who beat me at the charity race thing I did is going to be there. Please help me to beat her this time!

It's not that long now until the wedding. Mum said that if she and Peter didn't get married at the beginning of the summer holiday then they'd probably have to wait until next summer. Because Mum doesn't want a winter wedding. I still can't understand what all the hurry is about – they could easily wait a year, couldn't they?

I know that Peter's OK, Dad – he'd probably be one of your friends if he could be. But I still wish that Mum was getting married to you.

Lots of love, Suze

xxxxxxxxxxxxxxxxxxxxxxxxx

PS I wish you could kiss me back.

Chapter **Two**

'**But** what I don't understand is why they actually have to get married!'

I was in Cath's bedroom. It was getting towards the end of a fairly uneventful February half-term. We'd spent the morning in the local museum doing some research for a school project. Honestly – we *did* do it! Because it was all about costume for D&T and it was such a scrummy subject, we were really into it. We'd been at the museum all morning and now, after stuffing our faces with sandwiches, we were hanging out at Cath's.

I never knew Cath before we started secondary school together. I remember the day we started really well. We were all sitting in this enormous school hall. I was terrified – even though my cousin Ru was going to be in the same year. Of course, I did know some of the other kids from my primary school but even so, I felt really alone. Especially when Ru was called up into a class and I wasn't. Then I saw Cath. She was sitting in the row of kids in front of me and turned round. She looked as scared as I felt but she smiled at me. I smiled back. Then a woman started to call out our names, telling us which class we were in. I heard my name being called and went to stand with the teacher we'd been told to. Then I realised that Cath was joining the same class. The rest is history – we've been best friends ever since.

'So what's the big deal if they do get married?' Cath asked me. 'I mean, they spend loads of time with each other and Peter is there most weekends.'

'Exactly,' I said. 'Why do they need to change anything?'

'Because they love each other?' Cath suggested. 'Honestly, Suzy! Loads of kids at school have got stepdads, and they don't seem to be too stressed out because of it.'

Love – ouch, that hurt! Love – that was a bit scary. I mean, my mum loved *me*. My mum was always saying she still loved my dad. So how could Mum love Peter, too? If she had enough love left to love him, did that mean that she loved me and Dad a bit less each? Or perhaps she didn't really love Dad any more and was just saying it to make me feel better?

'Listen Suzy – you like Peter, don't you?'

'Well, yes.' I blinked.

'So what's the big deal? Anyway, your mum will buy you a new outfit for the wedding, won't she?' Cath said. 'And maybe some new shoes, too – so it's got to be worth it for that, hasn't it?'

I'd already been thinking about what I was hoping I would be able to get my mum to buy me, it was true. I'd also wondered if I would be able to get Mum to let me have a truly high pair of shoes I'd seen in Ravel. They were dead high. I wasn't convinced that Mum would agree but I had to try.

'True.' I smiled at Cath. 'And Peter's OK, really.'

'There you are, then,' Cath said.

'It's just the pits about Affie and Indie,' I wailed.

'Well, you won't have to live with them, will you?' Cath stood up. 'Oh stop moaning! Come on – let's see if we can persuade my mum to let us buy a Big Mac.'

We all went back to school on Monday. It was OK, I suppose. Not much to report – just the usual stuff. And, as I did on almost every day, I went back to Auntie Liz's with Ru.

'You going on that French trip, then?' I asked Ru.

'Dunno.'

'I'm going to try to persuade Mum to let me go.'

'Yeah.'

'You playing in the team this week then?'

Ru was really good at football. In fact, he was an all-round sportsman. Which was another reason why it was so odd that these days he hardly ever came out running with me and wanted to spend most of his time with his deadly dull mate Marco, playing computer games and watching the telly.

Silence. I tried again.

'So – you in the match this week? The one against St Michael's?'

'Humph.'

What did 'humph' mean? Yes? No? I don't care? I didn't make the team?

'Are you?' I persisted.

'What?' Ru's eyes didn't lift from the pavement.

We were turning the corner of his street and were only a short way from Auntie Liz's.

'In the team,' I said yet again. 'Are you in the team?'

'Dunno.'

And with that, Ru kicked the gate open and shoved his key in the door. He dumped his bag in the hallway and was up the stairs. He moved so quickly that the door was already closing on my face as I reached it. What was his problem?

'Ru? Suzy?' Auntie Liz called from the kitchen where I found her unpacking two bags of shopping. 'Hello love. How are you?'

'Fine, thanks, Auntie Liz.' I grabbed a bag and started to help her unpack the stuff.

I'd been in Auntie Liz's kitchen so many times that it was as familiar as my own. And in my house my mum would leave the bags on the table for ages before she got round to putting things away. It wasn't because she couldn't be bothered. It was because she would always have this brilliant idea about something she could do at school with a sauce bottle or something and get carried away with thinking about it. So, often as not, I'd end up shoving some of the stuff in the fridge myself.

'Oh thanks for that, sweetheart,' Auntie Liz smiled. 'Where's Ru, then?'

'Gone upstairs,' I explained. 'He seemed to be in a bit of a hurry. Couldn't even be bothered to speak to me, actually. So what's his problem these days?'

'Ru's?' Auntie Liz looked up at me from the kitchen cupboard. 'I don't think Ru actually needs a real problem to be in a mood these days. But if you find out what's up with him before I do, let me know, eh? I'm gasping – can you pop the kettle on for me?'

'Sure.'

When I'd done that, I sat down at the kitchen table and eyed a rather delish-looking cake that was sitting on the work surface. I wondered if I was going to be lucky enough to be offered some with my cup of tea. I was, as usual, starving.

'Ru?' Auntie Liz yelled up the stairs. 'There's a cup of tea and some cake down here if you want it.'

Result! I certainly didn't say no when it was offered to me a few seconds later. Choccie cake. With a great big dollop of chocolate fudge icing. Ru came into the kitchen and grabbed his tea and cake with a grunt. Then he went straight back upstairs again, saying nothing more than another grunt.

Weird. Once upon a time he'd have sat with me and Auntie Liz and we'd have talked about all sorts of stuff. We hadn't done that for what seemed like ages, though. Was it something I'd said, I wondered?

'So how's your mum?' Auntie Liz said, cradling her mug of tea in her hand.

'Fine, thanks,' I said. 'You know, busy with all the wedding stuff.'

'I expect she is,' Auntie Liz said, her back stiffening slightly as she kind of sat up a bit taller.

It was funny, but ever since Mum had announced that she was going to marry Peter, Auntie Liz's voice changed a bit when she was talking about Mum and Peter. It changed a lot when she was talking about Peter. Her voice kind of went sort of precise – pointed. Auntie Liz had always seemed to like Peter before – I mean, she'd even been round to us for barbecues and things when Peter was there and she'd seemed fine. But not since The Engagement. Since then, she'd started this voice thing.

'Mum wants everything to be perfect,' I explained. 'She's got lists for everything. Like she's dead organised.'

'Oh nothing will go wrong love,' Auntie Liz said, softening up again. 'Your mum is really good at organising things. I mean look how beautiful that classroom of hers always is!'

It was true. Mum just loved her job, and her classroom was like a showpiece classroom. Fab pictures all round the walls and loads of craft stuff everywhere.

'Auntie Liz?'

'Yes, love?'

'Doesn't Mum still love Dad?' Auntie Liz should know, I reasoned. After all, Auntie Liz was my dad's sister.

'Of course she does, Suzy.' Auntie Liz touched my arm with her hand.

'So how come she's got extra love for Peter, too?'

Auntie Liz was silent and thoughtful for a moment. Eventually she said, 'It's not extra love, Suzy. It's *more* love. She's got love for your dad, for you – oodles of it – and for Peter too.'

I looked at Auntie Liz and said nothing. It was like she was reading my thoughts for a bit and then she said, 'I don't know why things have to change, love, but for some reason they do. I mean, I still don't understand why your dad had to die. But he did. And he'd be so proud of you if he could be sitting here with us now. And I'll tell you something else, Suzy. If your dad was able to, he'd be saying that he loved your mum so much, he'd want her to be marrying Peter. *Because* he loved her so much. He'd want someone to love her back now that he can't do it himself.'

'D'you think?'

'I know so, Suze.' Auntie Liz squeezed my arm. 'I'd do anything to put your dad back in your kitchen and rewrite history. He was my brother, and I still miss him. I know it's in a different way from the way you and your mum miss him. But there's still a gap in my life, too.'

She paused for a bit and swallowed. She was almost crying and I felt bad because it must have been me asking her about all this that made her upset. Auntie Liz sipped her tea and then carried on. 'Suzy it wouldn't be right, though, if we all stayed living in the past, would it? Peter's a nice man. A good man. He's not going to let your mum forget about your dad. Honest.'

So is she right, Dad?
Was Auntie Liz telling me the truth? If she really doesn't mind about Peter why does she do all that posh voice stuff when she speaks about him? Would you honestly want Mum to be marrying Peter? If Mum had died instead of you, would I have a new mum? Would you be marrying Peter's ex-wife, Affie's and Indie's mum? I wonder what she's like? Do you think she's like Mum? I've never met her. Not that I want to.

Do you think that Peter is just like you, Dad? Honestly, I try to imagine what you and I would talk about when I come home from school every day. Would you come out running with me? Would you be going on at me about doing my homework every night? Or moaning like Cath's dad about what she wears? And would you still be calling me your princess? Would you call me princess in public? Yuck!

And did Mum go all gooey about your wedding like she is now?

LOL, Princess Suzy

Chapter **Three**

Disaster, Dad!

We had lunch at Peter's house today. Affie and Indie were there and it was just awful. I mean, if Affie was in my class at school there's no way she'd be one of my friends. She is so rude to everyone! Indie's not so bad but she's older and doesn't really want to hang around with me. And Peter goes all pathetic with Affie and Indie – even when they are rude! Affie's definitely the worse, though – no way do I want to spend time with her!

LOL, Suze xxxx

'So what do you think of this, Suze?' Mum asked me a few nights later.

'What's that?' I reached across the sofa and took the magazine from Mum. It was folded back to a picture of two girls in long bridesmaids' dresses. One dress was dark green and the other a rusty-red colour. Both of the girls had cheesy grins and flowers in their hair. They also had great big bunches of flowers in their hands.

'I thought you'd already chosen your dress?'

'I have darling, you know that,' Mum said. 'I'm just asking you if you like those dresses?'

'Well, if you've already chosen yours, what difference does it make whether I like them or not?'

Why do parents have to talk in riddles all the time?

'Well, thanks for being so helpful, Suzy!' Mum sighed. 'I just thought that you'd be happier if you chose your own dress, that's all.'

'What?'

Was I picking up a clue here? Was my mum making one of her unsubtle subtle hints? Was she suggesting what I thought she was suggesting?

'What do you mean, "what"?' Mum said, sounding irritated and tired.

'I meant, what dress? Der!' I replied, immediately regretting the sharpness in my voice and knowing that I couldn't do anything to swallow the words back.

'Your bridesmaid's dress, Suzy – that's what dress.'

I felt sick. 'You are not serious?'

'I beg your pardon, Suzy?' Mum snatched the

magazine back from me.

'You think I'm going to be a bridesmaid? Tell me you are joking!'

But it was obvious from my mum's face that she was deadly serious.

'You're expecting me to dress up in a girlie frock and have flowers in my hair?' I spluttered. 'You expect me to be a bridesmaid?'

Mum looked surprised and hurt by what I'd said. I felt guilty. But I also didn't want to be a bridesmaid.

'Well, Suzy, I had rather hoped that you would,' Mum said quietly. 'I thought it would be lovely for you to have a gorgeous dress and be there with me – a real part of the wedding. A way for you and Affie and Indie to join us properly. As a new family.'

My head was buzzing. If I hadn't already been sitting down, I probably would have fallen over – fainted.

'Now you really are joking!' I exclaimed. 'Me? Be a bridesmaid with Africa and India? No way!'

I put on this posh voice as I said their names and could see Mum wince as I did. She was making me feel bad by her reaction to my reaction. But not nearly as bad as the thought of having to dress up in a frock with those two girls.

'I thought you'd want to be my bridesmaid.

Obviously I shouldn't have assumed it was something that you'd want to do.'

She stood up and a wodge of bits of paper fell on to the floor as she did. She bent down to gather them up and I dropped to the floor to help her. From her superior position, Mum looked down at me and said, 'I wanted to include you in the day – thought you might want to support me. I hadn't realised that you'd feel so strongly against being a bridesmaid,' she said, sadly.

'Mum! I'm sorry – I didn't mean anything –'

But before I could finish, Mum had left the room and was slamming saucepan lids together in the kitchen as she made the supper.

'And this dress, right – it had all this shiny satin ribbon woven together across the boob bit. Disgusting or what?'

'Gross!' Cath giggled. We were sitting at lunch at school the next day. 'So what kind of dress are you going to have?'

'You what? No dress at all, of course! Do you honestly think I'm going to get dolled up in the same dress as Affie and Indie?'

'You going to go naked, then?' Cath raised her eyebrows.

'What you talking about?' I spluttered. 'Course not.'

'So what are you going to wear as a bridesmaid, then?'

'Bridesmaid?' I looked at Cath in amazement. Didn't she get it either? 'I'm not going to be a bridesmaid, you muppet.'

Cath looked at me, still shocked. 'You told your mum you weren't going to do it?'

'Course I did.'

'I don't believe you! She must have been so pissed off with you.'

I told Cath exactly what had happened the night before. 'But what I don't get Cath, is that you seem to think I would have said yes as well.'

'Well, you could have had a gorgeous dress. And shoes. And your hair done. And maybe some make-up too,' Cath tried to explain to me. 'If my mum was getting married, I'd want to be a bridesmaid.'

'I don't believe you,' I said. 'All fluffed up in some puffy dress that makes you look like a Barbie doll?'

'You don't have to look like that, you know,' Cath said. 'You could have had a really lovely dress that you could have kept afterwards.'

'Kept for what?' I wanted to know. 'For all the other occasions when someone wants me to be a bridesmaid for them? Like, hello? I don't think so.'

'So what's your mum said?' Cath asked.

'Not a lot since, really,' I explained. 'She's dead angry. I've really upset her.'

'I expect you have,' Cath said. 'You've got to change your mind. Say yes and be her bridesmaid.'

'I will not be a bridesmaid with Affie and Indie,' I said through slightly clenched teeth. 'I will not pretend that those stuck-up girls are really my friends.'

'Your sisters, you mean,' Cath said.

'*Step*sisters if you really must say it,' I pointed out. 'I thought you were my mate, Cath! Why are you getting at me as well?'

'I'm not getting at you, Suze! I just think your mum must be pretty upset by you. And I just don't understand why it is such a big deal to wear a bridesmaid's dress for a few hours.'

I glared at Cath across the table.

'But I do get the bit about Affie and Indie,' Cath added. 'Come on, Suze – let's not us argue about it, too. Fancy half my KitKat?'

'No,' I said. 'I fancy all of it!'

Peter came over for supper that night. Which was quite a good thing really because Mum was still being dead frosty with me. She was kind of speaking to me through

Peter. You know: 'Could you ask Suzy if she would like more beans?' That sort of stuff. And parents criticise their kids for being childish . . .

Peter did his best to make conversation. He asked me stuff about school and my next race. He even tried to chat with Mum a bit but she wasn't very cooperative. I knew that she'd told Peter about the argument when Peter said, 'I was talking with Affie and Indie late this afternoon.'

'Really?' Mum's voice was slightly clipped. 'How are they?'

'Very well. Very well indeed,' Peter said. 'I must say this salmon is delicious, Donna. Isn't it delicious, Suzy?'

'Er – yeah,' I said, wondering why he was asking for my opinion. I looked at him and he gave me this kind of conspiratorial look. I swear he almost winked at me.

'I was talking with Affie and Indie about the wedding earlier,' Peter continued.

'The wedding?' Mum's face changed, and she went from looking 'cross with Suzy' to 'I really should be looking cross with Suzy but now you're talking about my favourite subject, which makes me want to smile'.

'Yes,' Peter said. 'I was telling them about the latest plans and ideas. And I mentioned the possibility of them being bridesmaids.'

Peter's eyes didn't catch either Mum's or mine.

'Oh,' Mum said and put her fork down, waiting for his next word.

I didn't know what Peter was going to say next. I mean, if he said that they couldn't wait to be bridesmaids, I just might die.

'Affie and Indie were quite surprised,' Peter said, his eyes becoming fascinated with the pasta curls on his plate. 'And, of course, terribly flattered that you wanted them to be bridesmaids. Tremendously flattered, in fact.'

Thanks a lot Peter, I thought. Why not rub it in a bit more?

'But,' Peter went on.

But? But what? My ears were twitching.

'But they really felt – like I believe Suzy does – that they're perhaps a little bit too old to be bridesmaids now,' Peter concluded, obviously relieved that he'd got the message over with.

'Oh.' Mum put her fork down. 'So they don't want to be bridesmaids, either.'

She looked disappointed. Really disappointed. I felt a bit sorry for her.

'I wasn't laughing at your dress Mum – honest,' I said, truthfully. 'Its just . . . that . . . I mean, when do you ever see me in a dress?' Which was also truthful. I just didn't add the bit about not wanting to be seen dead in public with Affie and Indie. Natch. 'Especially a bridesmaid's dress.'

'Oh well – no bridesmaids, then,' Mum said.

I stood up and leant over the table to give Mum a hug. 'Forgive me?'

Mum hugged me back and then pulled away to look at me. 'Course.'

'So you'll buy me a fabby trouser suit to wear to the wedding instead, then?'

Laugh? Well, eventually she did.

Hi, Dad,

Result! I don't have to wear the dress and throw the confetti. Actually, I think it was Peter who helped me out over the Affie and Indie thing. You see, he told Mum how Affie and Indie don't want to do the bridesmaid thing, either. I think he understood how totally embarrassing it would be. And I didn't even have to say something gooey and suck up to him.

Can you imagine how dumb I would have looked all flowered up? Maybe you can't. You probably still imagine me as a little kid. Not the great lump I am now.

I wonder what you'd look like now, Dad? Would you have grey hair and wrinkles? Mum's got some grey hair but she dyes it in the bathroom every month. Would you have a beer belly like Uncle Joe? He always says it isn't a beer belly but a result of all Auntie Liz's delicious cakes. Could be. But he does drink loads of beer and Auntie Liz doesn't have a fat stomach.

Auntie Liz is a bit funny at the moment too, Dad. She's always seemed to like Peter. But now the wedding plans are being finalised it's like she doesn't really want to talk about it. Auntie Liz still loves you, Dad.

I love you too. Suze xxx

Chapter **Four**

The rest of the term went by really quickly. Mum got herself a second one of her crate things and started to keep some of her wedding stuff in it. But, being Mum, there were still piles of things all over the house. I carried on with my running training – without Ru, who hardly ever turned up to athletics club any more. I even managed to win a race in the inter-school championships at the beginning of the summer term. It was cool. Mum and Peter came to cheer me on – he took time off work to come to see it, and I was really touched by that. And, of course, I carried on writing to my dad.

We spent Easter at home, with Peter. We were meant to all go out to lunch with Affie and Indie, but they cancelled at the last minute because their mum decided to take them to Paris for the weekend. I could tell that Peter was disappointed. But, if I'm honest, I was relieved. After all, if they'd been with us, it wouldn't have been nearly so much fun and I couldn't have stuffed my face with so much chocolate.

When school went back, it wasn't much fun because we were all being crammed with information for our SATS. So it was relief when they were finally over and the teachers were less stressy . . .

'So where are you going to get this trouser suit then, Suze?'

We were sitting on a bench, hanging out at the park one afternoon. Cath had come to time me on a lap in preparation for my next race. Chilling out afterwards, I was gulping water and feeling quite pleased with my timing.

'Dunno,' I said. 'I thought we'd start in Top Shop and then cunningly try to push her towards Joseph. If I go greedy over the outfit too early, she might just change her mind.'

'Good point,' said Cath, who spent a lot of time with me trying to puzzle out how mums and dads clicked. 'But I bet you still thank Affie and Indie for getting you out of the fluffy dress situation.'

'You what?' I exclaimed. 'No way!'

'Give over, Suzy! If Peter hadn't spoken to them and found out how they felt about it, too, you might be in one of those wedding shops having pins stuck in you at this very moment!'

'Hmm,' I protested. I was never willingly going to admit that I was relieved that Peter's daughters had helped me out – big time. 'Hey, it's getting late. Better go, otherwise Mum'll be moaning about me being late for supper. She wants me to help her do the guest list.'

'OK, then.' Cath jumped up. 'Let's go.'

'Cauliflower cheese!' I sniffed and smiled as I walked into the kitchen. 'My fave! Hi, Mum!'

'Hello, darling!' Mum smiled. 'Have a good day?'

'Not bad – you got my message then?' I'd left a message on the answering machine from Auntie Liz's house about going for a run.

'I did darling – thank you. Oh sorry about that lot . . .'

Mum was standing stirring the cheese sauce at the cooker but she was nodding her head in the direction of all these loo roll tubes on the table. They were standing upright with bits of cotton wool and paper all jumbled around them. The glue stick had its lid off and, as usual, it was obviously Mum's school stuff being prepared for the next day.

'They're going to be pencil tidies,' Mum explained.

'You couldn't be a love and help put them in my crate, could you?'

'Sure,' I said, happy to try to create some order so that we could sit down to eat. I was, as usual, starving. 'Peter coming tonight?'

'Er, no,' Mum said, making me wonder if they'd had another row. Mum was so stressed about all the wedding preparations that she was more tetchy about everything these days.

'Peter's got a late work appointment – some contract that he's got to finalise. He said it would be best if he got a takeaway. He expects to be so late, you see. But he'll probably come here tomorrow.'

Peter seemed to work for all these really boring companies that bought and sold things all the time, and he was always doing these contracts. I had no idea what it was all about. It sounded complicated and boring to me. My dad hadn't done anything like that. My dad was a writer. He worked from home a lot of the time but he often used to go away on trips to do his research. At the time I had no idea what he used to research but we've got copies of all Dad's books in the tiny room upstairs that we jokingly call the 'study'. I've read all Dad's books over the last couple of years. Some of them are kind of history books, but they're really interesting because he wrote them all like they were stories. And some of the books are autobiographies – you see, my dad used to do ghostwriting for famous people. So that's why he was always doing research. I like to imagine that if he was here now, he'd be taking me on some of his trips to help him. Well, maybe. The day my dad died, though, he was going to see one of his publishers.

I don't know why I suddenly thought about Dad as I was clearing the table. I don't normally. Only when I'm writing my letters. I fast-forwarded my brain to the kitchen table and the here and now, and carefully placed Mum's precious craft things into the crate. My mum may have been chaotic in the way she did all these things, but she took such care of what she made.

'How's that?' I said, when everything was tidied away and sitting by the front door for the morning.

'That's wonderful, darling – thank you. Why don't you pop up and take a quick shower while I lay the table? We could have supper in about half an hour if that sounds OK?'

'I'll see you in twenty,' I replied. I needed to eat soon before I passed out with hunger!

'I thought we could go shopping to look at trouser suits for you,' Mum suggested as we both tucked in to our supper. Just like she was good at crafts, my mum was a fab cook, too. Between Auntie Liz and Mum, all my taste buds' desires were catered for.

'That'll be good – can I have some more?'

'Sure.' Mum stood up to dish up the extra. 'Um, Suzy?'

'Yeah?'

'Peter and I have been talking – about after the wedding.'

I munched away, waiting to hear what else she had to say. Especially as Mum looked a bit nervous. I could tell this because she'd stopped looking at me as she was talking. This is always a dead giveaway with adults.

'The problem is that Peter's got all his things in his flat . . . and we've got all our things here . . . and there isn't room in his place for all our stuff or room here for all his.'

'*His* flat?' I spluttered. Was my mum mad? Why on earth would we be interested in spending any time in Peter's flat? And why would we move any of our stuff to his place anyway?

Mum gave me a wary look. 'As I said – Peter's flat's too small.'

'Too small for what?'

'For us to move in there,' Mum explained.

'Course it is!' I'd been there for Sunday lunch once.

It was quite a nice flat. Quite posh, in fact. I'd been surprised actually how kind of trendy it was. 'So what's Peter going to do with all his stuff, then?'

'Bring it with him, of course,' Mum said. 'To our new house.'

The words sank into my ears and then started to whistle around them. *Ring* inside them.

'What new house?' I said. 'I thought we'd already decided that he was going to come and live with us here?'

'I know that we originally thought that, Suzy. But it's obvious – it's just too cramped here. Peter can't just get rid of all his stuff. And anyway, Affie and Indie will need somewhere to sleep when they come to stay.'

I froze. I'd kind of assumed that because the house was too small, we'd manage to avoid the Affie-and-Indie-coming-to-stay situation completely. Mum took a deep breath and carried on.

'We – Peter and I – thought it would be best to sell Peter's flat first and then put his things into storage while we sell this and look for a bigger place.'

I just glared at Mum.

'Suzy, darling – what's wrong?'

I still said nothing.

'It'll be fun, won't it? Having Affie and Indie to stay?' Mum said hesitantly.

Now I knew she was mad. Fun? Woof, woof! She was barking!

'Oh sure,' I mumbled. 'Like I'd rather run naked through school lunch . . .'

'Suzy!' Mum exclaimed. 'That's not a very nice thing to say.'

'Maybe not,' I said, slightly – but not much – under my breath. 'But it's the truth.'

'Affie and Indie are Peter's daughters,' Mum went on.

'Oh – and like I've had a chance *not* to notice that?'

'Of course you haven't,' Mum said. 'What kind of person do you think Peter would be if he didn't want to have his daughters round to where he lives?'

I stared at the ground, silently, my eyes stinging. Mum carried on talking at me.

'I cannot imagine not having you in my life every day Suzy. And Peter has to make do with only seeing his children on occasional weekends. And with Indie at university, he hardly sees her at all.'

Still I said nothing. Mum's words were ringing inside my head. I kind of knew that what Mum was saying was right – about Peter wanting to be with Affie and Indie. It was just hard to imagine that Peter would honestly want to spend that much time with someone as stroppy as Affie.

'Whatever,' I said, realising instantly that I just sounded sulky. 'I still don't want to leave here. Leave Dad's house.'

I looked up as I spoke and saw Mum wince as I said it. We were both silent for what seemed like ages. A couple of times, I thought Mum opened her mouth and then seemed to change her mind about what she was going to say. But eventually she said, 'I realise that it's a big change of plan, but we really will be much happier in a bigger house.' Mum reached across and put her hand around mine.

I snatched my hand away. 'But we can't move from here! This is our house! Dad's house! *My* dad's house! No – I'm sorry. You can move if you want to but I'm staying here!'

I texted Cath but she didn't get back to me. Her phone must have been switched off. Of course, Mum tried to talk to me. She'd followed me to my bedroom 'to explain'. But I didn't want to know! I liked our house. I'd always lived there and it was a good place. Stuff Peter's things! And what about my dad's ones? And stuff Affie and Indie coming to stay too!

I got my pen and paper out and started writing . . .

. . . and she says that Affie and Indie will be
coming to stay! Honestly, Dad, they are just
so stuck-up! And so kind of perfect. I can't
see them putting up with Mum's loo rolls
and yogurt pots! Not like I do. And anyway
– I don't want to share Mum with them!

Why does everything have to change all
the time? Who cares about having more
space? Anyway, if we don't have the space
then Affie and India can't come to stay!

I'm going to see if I can get Auntie Liz to
do something about it.

Love, Suze

I walked to school with Ru the next morning. I told
him all about it, as dramatically as I could.

'. . . I mean, how awful is that?' I was waving my
hands around in the air to emphasise my horror.

'You what?' Ru said.

'I said, how awful is that?'

'What?'

'Ru! Haven't you been listening to me?'

Ru looked at me blankly. Obviously he hadn't.

'Oh forget it!' I sighed and walked in through the
school gate. 'I'll see you later.'

I just didn't get it. Once Ru had been my best mate. As good a mate as Cath was. We talked about stuff. Had a laugh, even. I'd thought about it but I couldn't see that I'd done anything to upset him. Anyway, boys don't really get upset about stuff like girls, do they? These days Ru just didn't seem interested in anything I was interested in any more. All he was interested in was football and computer games. Geek.

Chapter **Five**

When Mum got home that night, she had loads of information about houses with her.

'How was school, love?' she asked, not giving me time to answer as she made a cup of tea. Clearly she wasn't really interested because she said, 'I've been busy reading these since I got home.'

She pushed some of the sheets of paper across the kitchen table at me. I was trying to do my homework and would have done anything for an excuse to stop. But no way was I going to let my mum think I was interested in her new house stuff.

'What do you think of this one? Peter and I think it's worth looking at,' Mum persisted. 'It's not far away – in Ascot Street. Isn't that near Cath's house?'

Of course it was – and Mum knew that! She was just trying to suck up to me. I didn't even look up and pretended to be rivetingly interested in my English homework. I heard Mum sigh and then she drank her tea while she looked at more of the house things. Every now and then she made some comment: 'Goodness – this one's got two bathrooms.'. . . 'Oh and this one's got a garage.' Like I cared? Like she cared if I cared? She was only interested in Peter's opinion really.

But eventually Mum got fed up with me. 'Oh please, Suzy! Please at least look at these things with me. Suzy?'

'I told you I don't want to move,' I muttered under my breath, not looking up from my homework.

'But I explained, darling – we just don't have enough space here for everyone.' Mum paused and then said, 'Even if Affie and Indie will only be staying for odd weekends. I promise you we won't move to somewhere that isn't at least as nice as this house.'

'You just don't get it, do you?' I spluttered, grabbing all my books. 'I like living *here*. OK?'

I went upstairs to my room.

I didn't like that night at home with Mum. I didn't like shouting at her. I never normally shout at her. Well, not much, anyway. I like my mum most of the time and didn't want to have a slanging match with her. But all she ever talked about was the wedding – and moving house. She hardly ever asked me about my running these days. I sat in my room feeling cross – cross with Mum and cross with myself for shouting at her. But I couldn't take the words back. No way was I going to back down and say I was sorry. Because I really didn't want to move.

Supper was yuck. Not the food but having to sit with Mum and Peter. He came round, like Mum said he would. And he tried to talk to me about my day at school. I didn't *want* to be rude to him. But I couldn't let him think that I was OK – OK about the house thing. I wanted him to realise that it was all *his* fault.

I think everyone was glad when I went upstairs to my room and stayed there until breakfast the next day.

Maddeningly, Mum and Peter both behaved as if nothing had been wrong the night before. No one mentioned the house, the strop – nothing. Both of them just smiled and talked about normal, breakfasty sort of things like what was on the radio and if it was going to be rainy or sunny that day. I'd kind of preferred it if they'd actually talked about it instead of pretending to be so cool about things. It was obvious that they'd had a row too. I'd heard them having it after I'd gone to bed. They don't shout and stuff when they argue –

maddeningly, because if they did I would hear what they actually said! But you can just make out these snappy-sounding voices and long, long silences from upstairs.

As soon as I could, I went round to Auntie Liz's to meet Ru. But when I got there, she seemed a bit surprised to see me and told me he'd already gone.

'He said you were going in on your own today,' Auntie Liz said. 'Sorry, love – I thought you'd made an arrangement.'

She looked a bit cross. I was pretty cross myself, but I didn't want to get Ru into trouble. I pretended like I'd just remembered something.

'Oh no! He's right – I'm meeting Cath! Sorry, Auntie Liz. Got to dash or I'll be late! See you later – bye!'

I ran to the bus stop and sure enough, Ru was already there. So was Cath. But then I usually met Cath at the bus stop – having walked there with Ru!

'Ru!'

Ru kind of looked round towards me but didn't look me in the eye. He just grunted and carried on with his Game Boy that he was playing with Marco. But I wasn't going to let him get away with it.

'You never told me you were going without me this morning,' I accused.

Still he said nothing.

'Ru – I'm talking to you! Why didn't you wait for me? You never said.'

'Give over,' Ru muttered, still not looking at me and barely pausing at the Game Boy.

'But we always come to school together!'

Marco and Ru started giggling and said nothing.

'I said, we always come to school together!'

'You might think that,' Ru said, not looking up. 'But I've changed my mind.'

'Changed your mind?' I spluttered, feeling hurt because he was rejecting me. 'Since when? And why?'

'Because I just don't want to any more – get a life, Suzy!' Ru sniggered at me. Marco laughed.

I could feel the blush start at my shoes and work up to my scalp. It was *so* humiliating. I'd come to school with Ru for ever and now he was just laughing in my face. In public. He wasn't just my friend; he was my cousin. He was supposed to be on my side.

'Leave it, Suze,' Cath whispered in my ear. 'It's his problem. Just ignore him.'

I kind of knew she was right but it still hurt. I was glad when the bus turned up and Cath and I could sit at the other end from Ru and Marco.

* * *

'But what was it all about?' I whined at Cath when we got off the bus.

'Does he need a reason?' she said. 'He's a boy, isn't he? Boys are just weird. They spend all their time doing drossy things and thinking that their jokes are just about the funniest things in the world. Oh – and when they aren't doing that, they're farting and burping.'

I had to laugh. I mean – it was perfectly true of most of the boys in our class. And the ones who didn't behave like that were the swotty ones who always put their hands up first when the teacher asked a question.

'But he wasn't always like that,' I tried to explain. 'He used to be really friendly. A good laugh.'

'And you used to have plaits and play with Barbie,' Cath said. 'Listen, don't take it personally. He's just a boy, after all. Anyway – it's his loss if he wants to hang around with Marco all the time.'

'Suppose so,' I mumbled. But I wasn't that convinced. Not even by Cath.

Dad!
Why does all this poo have to keep happening? First of all Ru has gone off me and won't speak to me any more – all he wants to do is hang about with that drongo

Marco and count his zits! He's just no fun any more. And secondly – it gets worse! Not only does Mum say we have to leave this house and go and live in some other drossy place somewhere else with Peter, but now she says we're going to have Affie and Indie over for lunch on Sunday because we're going to celebrate Peter's birthday. It is just so not fair!

They're all coming over here at the weekend – and Mum thinks I'm going to help her cook! Like, hello?

Love, Suze

Chapter **Six**

Mum was in a twitch all weekend. She'd spent the rest of the week pawing through cookery books and asking what I thought Affie and Indie would like to eat. Like I cared?

'We have to try to get on. I mean,' Mum said as she hysterically wrote her shopping list, 'once we all get to know each other better, see more of each other, we can all be friends. Sunday's a good chance for us to find out more about each other.'

Friends? From where I was, I somehow doubted we'd be friends. Of course, I know Mum was so twitched because it was the first time she'd actually cooked a proper meal for them. Every other time, it had either just been something like a cake for tea or Peter had taken us out to eat. Mum even tried to drag me off to the supermarket to get the food with her. But I managed to use the excuse that I needed to go out running to get out of that one, though I did help her ice the cake.

By Sunday morning, Mum was behaving as if she was at school and about to be inspected – she was so stressy! Peter went off to go to collect Affie and Indie in the morning, and while he was gone I helped to lay the table. To be honest, it seemed easier to help than to make a fuss. Mum was so twitched. I felt sorry for her. It was only Affie and Indie, for goodness' sake – they weren't worth it. When I'd finished, I went up to my room and called Cath.

'So what are you wearing?' she asked.

'My jeans and fleece.'

'Making an effort, then?' Cath laughed.

'Well, they're not going to be interested in what I wear, are they?' I replied defensively.

'I'd have thought that they'd be really interested myself, but it's up to you.'

Was she serious? I hoped not.

'Mum's freaked out by the whole thing. The kitchen's a disaster area of mixing bowls and saucepans!'

'Well, at least you know the food will be deelicious!'

Which was true. My mum may be a messy cook, but even when she's stressed she's a really good one.

'Oh – I think I can hear Peter's car,' I said, jumping

up and going over to my bedroom window. 'It is . . . they're here.'

'Better go then,' Cath said. 'Enjoy!'

'Oh – as if!' I sighed.

I left it as long as I possibly could before I went down. Peter was all kind of stiff and not nearly as friendly with me as he usually was. I was irritated when he smiled at me when Affie and Indie weren't looking. Why was everyone so scared of these girls? Mum was just as bad, almost ignoring me and she kept giggling nervously every time she said something. And that was a lot because she just didn't *stop* talking. 'Who wants something to drink? He he!' . . . 'Any one hungry? Hope so – he-he!' . . . 'Would you like to sit down? He-he!' . . . 'Want to stand up? He he!'

In between Mum waffling on, Affie and Indie didn't say much, except to answer Peter when he spoke to them and when Affie muttered occasional things to Indie under her breath for no one else to hear. I knew the instant I saw them that I'd got the jeans and fleece bit wrong. Affie was wearing an amazing pair of jeans with patterns all over the fronts. She had a T-shirt with mirrors and embroidery on it and a matching cardigan. She also had a pair of sparkly flip-flops that I would have told Cath were gorgeous if she was wearing them.

But I wasn't going to say that to Affie.

Indie was wearing a dress that was all floaty and soft and she also had sandals to die for. She looked stunning. And I hated them both for making me feel like a dross.

When we sat down to eat, Peter and Mum did most of the talking – or at least Peter tried to talk when Mum occasionally stopped for breath. She kept bombarding Affie and Indie with questions: about school and university and what their hobbies were. Had my mother gone mad? Hobbies? Like she thought Affie and Indie collected porcelain boxes? Or stuck things in scrapbooks?

Indie was loads nicer than Affie. She kept telling Mum how nice the food was and asked her all about her job. Mum asked about their mum and it turned out that she's a barrister. I'd probably been told that before, I know, and Mum must have known it but she still hadn't learned to put her mouth on hold. That was one of the only times that Affie said much, when she was talking about her mother. She kept saying how smart she was and how she'd got to the top of her profession and was always in the paper for winning cases in court.

'What about your father, Susannah?' Affie suddenly said, when she'd stopped showing off about her mum. 'What does he do?'

Peter coughed. Mum winced and looked at me with eyes that told me she wanted to give me a hug. I did not, for one minute, think that Peter had not explained about Dad. Especially as Affie had never mentioned my dad when I had met her before. Indie, though, looked daggers at Affie and looked as if she had given her a kick under the table.

'It's Suzy – not Susannah,' I said, putting my spoon down in my pudding bowl. 'And, as I thought you already knew, my dad pushes up daisies. Anyone want any more pudding?'

I felt my cheeks flush with irritation and anger. And boy, was I angry. What business was my dad to Affie?

'You mean your father is a gardener?' Affie said, her nose turned up as if she could smell dog poo. How horrid could this girl be? I was certain that Peter had told her about my dad.

'No,' I said, looking down at my plate and thinking what a bitch she was. 'My dad's dead. That's how he manages to push daisies up.'

'Would anyone like some tea or coffee?' Mum asked, jumping up from her seat.

They left after tea, which was a relief for us all. Peter drove them home and left me and Mum to tidy things away. Tea itself was OK. Affie and Indie seemed gobsmacked when they realised that we'd made the cake ourselves. They obviously never did things like that in their house. Indie kept on saying how delicious the cake was and how clever we were to have done it. Affie just sulked. Before they left, Indie tried to apologise to me on Affie's behalf. Which I thought was quite decent of her. I felt sorry for Peter. After all, it was his birthday.

'It wasn't really Affie's fault,' Mum said as we loaded the dishwasher.

'Huh. She knew full well.'

'It will get easier,' Mum continued. 'Once we're all friends, things will be more relaxed.'

'They could hardly be more tense, could they?' I pointed out. 'They're so posh! They're nothing like us.'

'But they're Peter's daughters,' Mum said.

'So?'

'So they must be like him – when you get to know them better.'

'Course – but Affie and Indie must be loads like their mum because he's loads more normal than they are!'

'Suzy! Don't be so rude!' Mum said and then laughed. 'Blimey – they were rather stunning, weren't they? Their clothes! Can you imagine what their mother looks like?'

'I think I can,' I smiled. 'But I don't think she can bake a cake, do you?'

We giggled together and then Mum gave me a hug.

'I've been thinking,' she said afterwards. 'About the wedding.'

'Well, there's a surprise!' I said, and we both laughed.

'As I was saying,' she said, smiling. 'I was wondering if you would like Cath to come to the wedding with you? Someone for you to be with?'

I grinned. 'Thanks, Mum. I'd like that a lot!'

Dearest Dad,

I don't think it could have been more awful! But I'm also a bit ashamed. I don't think I helped make this much better – and it couldn't have been a very nice birthday for Peter either. Which wasn't very nice of me for Mum either. Sorry, Dad.

What's it going to be like when we move? Affie turned her nose up at everything here. I could see her doing it – like we were saddos and she was posh. I've seen Peter's flat – it's all smart furniture and no clutter. It is posh, like Affie and Indie. You know our house isn't like that! Our house has old things – comfortable things. Your things, Dad. I've only ever lived here – and I've always been round the corner from Auntie

Liz's. I won't be able to go back to her every afternoon if we don't live here.

Every room in this house reminds me of you, Dad. I know we've redecorated some of the rooms and things like that since you went. But we haven't changed any of the furniture. And I haven't changed my bedroom. And we've still got your desk in the spare room (although it's full of Peter's stuff as well) – the desk where you used to do all your work. We've even got your old typewriter still. Sometimes I go and sit at your desk, Dad, and think about you. I sit in your old comfy desk chair and look around at all your books and things – your notebooks. And I breathe in the air and it smells of you. Like you are still here.

I really don't want to move, Dad.

Love you loads, your princess. Xxxxxx

Chapter **Seven**

There was so much going on in the last few weeks of the summer term. At school we had loads of school trips and concerts and stuff. Mum was doing all those things, too, and making the final plans for the wedding. She was so involved with the wedding when she was at home that she'd stopped talking about moving. Fortunately, Mum and Peter had announced that selling our house was one too many hassles to cope with on top of the wedding. They'd handle that, they said, once the wedding was over. But Peter did say that he had put his own flat up for sale. I'd asked him what he was going to do with all his furniture, and he'd told me that it was going off to some warehouse until we found a bigger house for us all to move to. So if his furniture was definitely coming to the new house, where was all our furniture going to go, I wondered?

Mum had wedding lists all over the house: who was

invited and whether they had said yes; what time everything was due to happen; who the photographer should take photos of; what food was being served; everything.

'I don't understand why she's in such panic stations about the thing,' I said to Auntie Liz one afternoon. 'I mean, it's not like she hasn't organised a wedding before, is it?'

Auntie Liz smiled and said, 'Well, actually, she hasn't really, Suzy.'

This was news to me! Was she trying to tell me that my mum and dad had never actually been married and I'd been misled all these years? This made life a whole load more interesting – and me, too!

Auntie Liz was reading my thoughts. 'It's nothing like that Suzy.' She laughed.

'Tell me more.'

'There's not much to tell, really,' Auntie Liz explained. 'You see, your mum and dad had a bit of a whirlwind romance. They met at college – but it was only when they were graduating that they went out together and fell in love. A few weeks after they left college, they went to Scotland for a holiday. And when they came back, they were married.'

'What – just like that?' I was surprised.

'Yes.' Auntie Liz smiled a kind of dreamy smile. 'It was very romantic – although your gran didn't think so at the time! Nor did Donna's mother. They'd decided to get married while they were away and went to Gretna Green to do it.'

'So it was dead romantic?'

Auntie Liz laughed. 'Yes – it was, Suzy. But everyone gave them such a hard time when they got home. People said it wouldn't last because they hadn't known each other for long enough. That they were too young.'

'But it did last!' I said defensively.

'It did,' Auntie Liz said. 'They were very happy – the perfect couple.'

We sat in a kind of happy-sad silence for a while. Then Auntie Liz broke it and said, 'So you see, your mum may have had a romantic wedding in some ways before, but she's never had the wedding dress and the photographs – all that kind of stuff.'

'So that's why she's so worried about it all,' I said.

'Think so,' Auntie Liz said, taking my hand and squeezing it. 'I think we'd all best make sure it's a happy day for her and Peter, don't you?'

Just then Ru stumbled into the kitchen and grunted some words that Auntie Liz seemed to know meant

'When are we going to eat?' She told him and then he grunted some more and went to his room.

Weird.

Mum and I finally got to go shopping for my wedding outfit and we had quite a giggle. I persuaded Mum to buy me a really cool pair of trousers. She'd also bought me a jacket. I'd changed my mind about having the trouser suit because it made me look like a policeman when I'd tried it on in the shop. What Mum had bought me made me feel much more like me. Mum looked really nice in a dress that she'd bought and she had these really great shoes – nothing like the sort of thing she would normally wear. She looked so happy – so did Peter. It would have been difficult not to be happy for them. And I was.

I'd thought a lot about what Auntie Liz had said that time about not living in the past. Mum deserved to have someone like Peter to love her. As well as me.

The wedding was at some big house, just outside town. Cath and I went there in Uncle Joe's car with Auntie Liz and Ru. It was a pain being squashed up in the back seat with Ru who made it clear that he'd much rather be playing football with Marco. Until we got there, that is, and he saw Affie and Indie.

Affie and Indie were standing around waiting in the shade outside the house. It was a really hot sunny day.

'Check out those outfits!' Cath exclaimed when she saw them.

They were both wearing fantastic clothes. Both in dresses with these gorgeous embroidered chiffon cardigans. Not that they were in twee twin outfits or anything ghastly like that. Each of them looked quite different, really. And both of them looked fab. And to make it worse, they both had these to-die-for tans.

'Oh disgusting!' I hissed, when I saw Ru's reaction to them. 'He's practically dribbling!'

Cath laughed. It was true! His mouth had dropped open and he could hardly keep his eyes off them. 'Gross!' Cath said.

Ru followed Affie and Indie around the whole afternoon. I noticed that he managed to think of things to speak with *them* about! How unfair is that? He hadn't spoken more than two words to me for weeks – months! Now he had his tongue hanging out and was falling all over them.

Cath and Auntie Liz made me go and speak to Affie and Indie after the service bit was over. Just like she had been at lunch all those weeks before, Indie was chatty –

she told us all about how she was going to spend the summer working in France at a camp site. She was quite nice, really, and she even said she thought my mum looked really nice. I noticed that Affie didn't agree with her. She was just pouting – except when she kept grabbing Peter's arm as if he was her property and she wasn't going to let him speak to other people.

There was a cringe-making moment when the photographer said he wanted to take a picture of the three of us. Indie stood in the middle and cracked jokes. I began to think that maybe she was OK, really. At least her jokes were funny and made me smile for the photographs. But Affie didn't want to have any of it. She even moaned when it was time to have our photograph taken with Mum and Peter.

'The new family together!' the photographer said.

That made me feel a bit sick. Now Affie and Indie were officially my stepsisters.

Then it was time for all the speeches and stuff. Peter made one saying how happy he was to have three daughters now and Auntie Liz squeezed my arm. Oh please! Then Mum made a speech saying how happy she was and stuff. But she didn't mention my dad, I noticed.

She'd almost finished when there was all this fuss behind her and Mum forgot what she was planning to say. Everyone turned to where all the noise was coming from. It was Affie – of course! She said that she'd burned herself on a candle as she was trying to get some food. Like – yeah, right. She was just trying to get some attention! Baby. Even at a time like this, she had to demand attention. Peter looked a bit flustered about it but India dragged her off to the Ladies. I like to think she gave her an earful – but who knows? Mum just smiled her way through it, like she was her own personal cloud of happiness.

She'd arranged for a girl to play the flute during the reception. She'd discovered her busking outside the supermarket one day and started to chat with her. She was a music student – typical of Mum to make friends. But the girl, Tilly, was really good, and you could hear her in the background as everyone chatted. All Mum's friends from school were there and they kept telling me how nice I looked. Auntie Liz and Uncle Joe rather embarrassingly told them how proud of me they were.

But then before we knew it, the wedding was over and it was time for Mum and Peter to go off on their honeymoon. Peter had refused to tell anyone – even Mum – where they were going. He'd just asked her to pack things for a warm country. We all went outside where there was a car waiting to take them to the airport.

'Suzy? Suzy, darling?' Mum was looking for me.

I rushed over to her. 'Hey, Mum,' I said, feeling like I was about to cry. It was so embarrassing! I hadn't thought I'd feel like this! What kind of blubber baby was I? 'Love you, Mum. Have a wonderful time. Send me a postcard.'

How pathetic was I? Send me a postcard? That was the best I could do?

'Love you too, Suzy. Loads, you know that?'

'Course,' I said, sniffing and wishing I had a hanky. 'Stop it, Mum, or your mascara will run. Go on – go before the plane leaves without you!'

Over Mum's shoulder I could see Affie and Indie saying goodbye to Peter.

He gave me a hug as he said goodbye to me.

Then they got in the car and they were off. My whole life had changed. Again. Changed for ever and I suddenly felt blubby and empty.

'Give me a hug,' Auntie Liz said. 'After all, I need one and Ru won't give me one any more so you've got no choice.'

I could tell that she was fibbing (well, maybe not about the Ru bit) but I was relieved that she seemed to know how I felt without really having to say anything.

I spent the rest of the reception hanging around with Cath, not saying very much at all.

Dear Dad,
I really love you so much. Mum looked beautiful today. You'd have been really proud of her. I know I've got a stepdad as well now, Dad, but I'll never, ever, stop loving you.
Love, Suze, xxx

Chapter **Eight**

For the next three weeks I stayed at Auntie Liz's house. Mum and Peter had rung from their hotel when they'd arrived to say they were in the Seychelles and that it was fab and she'd send us a postcard. Auntie Liz was, as usual, great and we did some really good things like going to London. We saw some cool films and even had some fun trying to do some nail art on Auntie Liz.

When I wasn't with Auntie Liz I went over to Cath's as often as I could so that I could avoid Ru. To be honest, I'd begun to almost dislike him. If he wasn't lying around in a kind of coma, he was playing stupid kids' games with Marco. And every time Ru and Marco saw me, they just collapsed into giggles about some private joke that felt like it was about me. Geeks.

It was a hot summer, so we spent as much time in the garden as we could. When we weren't just hanging out there, we sat in the cool shade of Cath's old tree house and read. And, of course, I did my running.

Every other day, Auntie Liz and I went back to our house to check that everything was OK. It seemed strange going back to an empty house. It was musty from the heat, and we always opened up the back door to let some fresh air in. Sometimes Auntie Liz made us a cup of tea and we sat in the garden drinking it.

She was boiling the kettle one afternoon while I was sorting the heap of post that I'd found on the doormat. There was the obvious stuff that was rubbish – Mum had already said I could just throw it straight away – and then some postcards from some of her workmates from school who'd been at the wedding and had written from their holidays. OK – so I read Mum's mail, but I couldn't resist it. And they were postcards – even the postman could have read them. I was a bit startled, though, when I got to the bottom of the pile and there was a letter addressed to Peter. At our house. Our house that was now his house, too.

As if she sensed my feelings, Auntie Liz said, 'Any postcard from your mum and Peter yet?'

'Er – no.'

'Oh, well – perhaps the post is bad where they're staying,' she said.

'Maybe the postcard will get here after they do!' I said.

In fact, it didn't. We got a postcard from Mum and Peter (she wrote it and they both signed it) the day before they got back. It was a beach scene.

'How swanky is that?' Auntie Liz said. 'I bet they've had a fabulous time.'

'I hope so.' I smiled. I couldn't wait to see Mum. And, nice as Auntie Liz was, I couldn't wait to get back home and away from Ru and Marco.

The day they came home, I spent the morning in the house. I felt excited, almost as if I'd been on holiday myself. With Auntie Liz, I opened the windows in the bedrooms and whizzed round dusting and polishing. I even got the Hoover out! Then we went into the garden and picked some flowers to put in a vase. Actually, we did two – one for the hall and the other one for the kitchen.

'Suzy!' Mum rushed in to the house when she got out of the taxi and came straight up to me.

'Mum! You look great!'

She did, too. She was relaxed and smiley. She didn't have a bling-bling tan, but she did have a kind of glow. Part of the glow was happiness, I could tell.

'Hello, Suzy!' Peter said, coming into the house with their suitcases. 'Doesn't this place look great?'

'Hi, Peter.'

He put the bags down and gave me a hug. 'It's really good to be home.'

'I'm really looking forward to a lovely cup of tea,' Mum said.

'Let's have some in the garden,' I suggested, thinking of all the afternoons that Auntie Liz and I had had over the last few weeks. 'Auntie Liz has made us a cake.'

'Even better!' Peter said.

'There's some post for you. Both of you,' I said, handing over the two separate piles I'd made in the kitchen. 'You want some tea, Auntie Liz?'

'Actually, I'd better be getting back,' she said. 'Come and see me soon, eh Suzy?'

'Are you sure you won't stay?' Mum asked. 'We can't eat your cake without you.'

Auntie Liz smiled. 'Honestly – no. It's lovely to see you both. Why don't we catch up on things one afternoon next week?'

Then she left. And the three of us sat in the garden, while Mum and Peter told me all about the Seychelles.

The next day was Sunday and it was Peter's last day before he went back to work. It was a hectic one because he brought some of his things over from his flat.

There were loads of work files that he filled Dad's tiny study with – the room that Mum sometimes jokingly called the spare bedroom. I noticed, though, that Peter didn't put anything on Dad's desk. But Mum's bedroom – Mum's and *Peter's* bedroom was suddenly stuffed with clothes. It was like a nightmare and I was glad that my room wasn't like that. Honestly, if anything else was put in our house, it was going to go pop.

Dad!
Guess what? Peter has put your old desk in my room! We had to try to make some space in the study for some of his boxes and things – things he couldn't put into storage because he needs them most days. So then Mum said why didn't I have your desk? So I have. And your old chair – the one that twists round.

I've polished them both up and put my PC on the desk. It's really cool. In fact, it's where I'm sitting while I write this. I was putting my things in the drawer, Dad, and I found a piece of paper tucked in at the back. It was a story I wrote for you at school! I did it for you when I first went to school and it was for Father's Day. You should have seen the spelling mistakes! And it had your handwriting on the bottom. It said my name and the date. I can't even remember doing it. Is that really bad of me? I folded it up and put it back in the drawer. It's still there in the same place that you put it.

Love you, Dad. Suze xxxxxx

Chapter **Nine**

I had a really good day with Mum on the Monday. I'd missed her so much while she'd been away that even doing drossy things like going to the supermarket were good fun. I didn't even mind when Mum told us all about her trip all over again when Cath came round in the afternoon. But then Mum started whittering on about the piles of house information that had come while she'd been away. So I took that as a chance to escape, leaving her to read them all while I took Cath upstairs to show her dad's desk.

'Isn't it cool?'

Cath looked at it. 'Not bad. I mean, it's kind of cool in a kind of old sort of way.'

'Exactly,' I said, feeling pleased. 'Problem is, it's a bit crowded in here now.'

'You certainly won't be able to have too many parties in here,' Cath joked. 'But then, when you move you'll get a bigger bedroom anyway.'

'Suppose,' I thought aloud.

'I wish I was going to have a bigger bedroom,' Cath said. 'You're dead lucky being able to start all over again with a new place and all that fun of decorating it the way you want.'

'Yeah – I suppose I am,' I said and sighed.

We were eating supper with Peter that night when the phone rang.

'Hello?' I said.

'It's Affie. Fetch me my father please.'

And hello and how nice to speak to you too! I thought. Oh well, at least she said please, I suppose . . .

I passed the phone over to Peter. 'It's Affie for you.'

Peter smiled and thanked me before he took the phone from me.

'Hello, sweetie,' he said and then went into the hallway to carry on the conversation.

Mum looked at me and smiled but didn't say anything. As we carried on with our meal, you could hardly hear Peter speak. He seemed to be doing more listening. But every now and then we could hear him say, 'Don't worry, sweetie. I'll do it.' Obviously Peter was going to be busy doing all the things that Affie wanted him to do.

A few minutes later, he was back at the table. 'Erm, I've got to go and collect Affie from her friend's.'

'What, now?' Mum said.

'Yes. Her mother was going to fetch her but she's been delayed at work. It's not a good idea for her to travel on the bus at this time of night. It won't take me long.'

'Course not,' Mum said, slightly stiffly I thought. 'When's Affie going to come and see us? It would be lovely to show her the photographs of the honeymoon.'

I just carried on eating. I didn't want to be part of this.

'Why don't I ask her to come this weekend?' Peter suggested.

And, can you believe it, Mum agreed!

'You've got to help me out,' I begged Cath on the phone later that night. I was sitting on my bed, looking out of the window, and I'd just told her about Affie. 'Please let me come over and spend the day with you?'

'Your mum'll never stand for that – and you know it.'

'Why not?'

'Like you really need me to tell you? For the obvious reason that you and Affie are meant to get to know each other and you are hardly going to do that if you aren't there, are you?'

'Don't get so stressy with me!' I moaned.

Cath laughed. 'Tell you what. Why don't I come over on Saturday afternoon and see how you are all getting on?'

'You'd better!' I said.

Dear Dad,

Affie is coming tomorrow. I spent the afternoon with Mum, getting things ready for her. Honestly, you'd think it was the Queen coming to stay. The fuss! Peter's getting all twitched about it and so is Mum. She's even been cleaning the leaves on the houseplants! Like since when did Mum care about stuff like that?

I thought Affie would be sleeping in the study. But when Mum and I tried to get the camp-bed thing all fixed up in there, we couldn't make it fit. Disaster! Because Mum said that Affie will have to share my room. I told here there was no way and my room wasn't big enough either. But Mum says I've got no choice – until we move house, anyway. She said that I was always able to find room when Cath slept over. Which is true. But that's different! And, anyway, Cath hasn't slept over since I got your desk in my room. So I told Mum that I didn't like Affie and I didn't want her any where near my room. Mum said that I didn't know Affie well enough to know that I did not like her. What does Mum know?

Love, Suze xxxxxxx

Peter drove over to collect Affie early on Saturday morning. Indie wasn't coming, of course, because she'd already left for France. Lucky her. As I could have predicted, Affie was frosty with me and Mum from the start. We had coffee in the garden and then Mum suggested that we all went in the car to the river so that we could walk along the towpath and then have lunch in a pub there.

'But Mum!' I protested. 'Cath's coming over this afternoon!'

'Well, that won't stop us from going out this morning, will it?' Mum replied. 'Give Cath a call and say that we'll collect her on our way back. Then how about we make a cake for tea?'

'OK,' I sighed.

Affie spent most of her time just looking at us. It was weird. Like she was inspecting us. Like we didn't meet her approval.

When we got to the river, Mum and Peter were chatting away about stuff – houses, mainly, of course – and Mum gave me a bag of old bread to throw at the ducks. She suggested that Affie and I did it together. But Affie looked at her as if she was mad. Clearly, feeding the ducks was far too babyish and un-cool for someone like Affie. So I fed the ducks on my own.

Over lunch, Peter and Mum tried to tell Affie all about their trip, but she made it completely obvious that she simply wasn't interested. She just didn't want to know. The only time her eyes lit up, was when she was speaking to Peter. She called him 'Dads' in this kind of babyish way and kept snuggling up to him. And when we walked back to the car later, she held his hand like she was a little girl.

Poor Mum. I could tell that she was feeling kind of left out. Or maybe pushed out, even. But she dropped back – kept her distance, even. Like she didn't want to interfere. I felt sorry for Peter too, though, because he looked so uncomfortable. So like he didn't want it all to be happening.

'Well, at least you're going to get a peaceful night's sleep,' Cath said as she was leaving much later that evening. She'd tried to chat with Affie as well, and Affie had made it clear that she wasn't interested either. 'Unless she snores!'

We both giggled helplessly.

'It's a nightmare!' I moaned. 'Can I sneak back to your place with you?'

'You can't desert your mum!' Cath laughed. 'Anyway – she'll be gone tomorrow!'

'I can't wait!' I sighed.

Chapter Ten

Back in the kitchen, I grabbed another piece of the remains of the cake we'd made for tea (coffee cake with walnuts on the top) and was stuffing my face with it when Mum came in to the kitchen.

'I need this,' I said, making an excuse for myself. 'The energy – I'm going on a run in a minute.'

Mum laughed. 'Peter's going to do a barbecue this evening,' she said, nodding her head in the direction of the garden, where he was busy trying to light the thing. I couldn't see Affie with him, though. Which was odd because she'd stuck to him like a limpet for the entire day. 'So you'd better not be out for too long.'

'Where's Affie?'

'Oh – she's gone upstairs to have a shower,' Mum said, grabbing things from the fridge. 'So she'll be out well before you need one when you're back.'

'Sure,' I said.

I didn't like the idea of Affie being upstairs in my house. Upstairs, alone. Where I couldn't see her. I swallowed the last crumbs of cake and went upstairs to my room to change in to my running gear.

'What the . . .?' I exclaimed aloud as I got on to the landing and got a view of my bedroom. It was a dump. A total tip! A trail of clothes was on the floor and I could see there were more clothes on my bed and loads of bottles and other stuff on the chest of drawers. Affie's bag was on top of Dad's desk.

I stood, staring helplessly at the chaos. I couldn't believe that Affie could treat my room like this – how dare she?

'Oh – it's you,' Affie said as she came across from the bathroom. She had her towel wrapped around her and didn't seem to be remotely embarrassed either by what she looked like or what she'd done.

I was still speechless when Affie calmly sat down on my bed in her damp towel and started to comb her hair. What did she think she was? Some kind of mermaid?

Eventually I said, 'What's all this lot?'

'Oh I know,' Affie said. 'It's just so cramped in here, isn't it? It must be really hard for you all to have to live in such a small house. I feel really sorry for you.'

'Cramped? It wasn't cramped until you dumped this lot everywhere,' I exploded, lying about the

82

place not being cramped before.

'Well, where else can I put it?' Affie said defiantly. 'Stressy!'

'Well . . .' Irritatingly, I kind of agreed with Affie. But it was all her clobber that made it cramped.

'Everything all right?' Mum said, sounding worried as she came up the stairs. 'Oh . . .'

Mum stood and looked at the pair of us. She opened her mouth as if she was going to say something and then closed it, obviously changing her mind. I reckoned even someone as messy as Mum could see that my room was looking way out of order.

'I'm going for a run,' I said, grabbing my trainers and not bothering to put my shorts on.

'Don't be long, darling,' Mum said anxiously. 'Peter will need to start cooking soon.'

It was a relief to pound out my anger on the pavement! After half an hour, I'd thumped my feet so hard I felt like I'd run for hours. I was exhausted when I got back home.

'Hello, love.' Mum smiled sheepishly at me. 'Good run?'

'Fine, thanks, but I need a shower,' I explained, wiping the sweat from my brow with my sleeve. It had been a mistake not to have changed.

As I walked to the stairs, Affie came out of the living room. She didn't even disguise her horror at what I looked like with my flushed face. Much as I hated her, I was embarrassed at having great big sweat marks under my arms.

Upstairs, I closed the bathroom door, glad of the privacy. After undressing, I went over to open the shower door.

'Yuck!' I exclaimed as my bare feet made contact with the shower mat. It was soaking wet – with Affie's cold water. I opened the shower door and stepped in. 'Oh gross!'

Judging by the amount of hair on the cubicle floor and in the plughole, Affie wasn't used to cleaning up after herself.

Somehow we managed to get through the rest of the weekend. Completely out of character, Mum suggested that we all went swimming together on the Sunday morning. Going swimming together was simply not something we normally did. Affie made this huge fuss about how she couldn't possibly go because she didn't have a costume with her and, anyway, she'd only just washed her hair. Peter shut her up quickly by saying that he would buy her a costume at the pool and she could always wash her hair again, like she did every day.

Actually, being at the swimming pool was quite good fun, because we didn't really need to speak to each other as we ploughed up and down doing our own thing. And Affie was obviously very pleased with herself because when Peter had taken her to the sports shop at the pool she'd managed to get him to buy her the most expensive costume they had.

When we got back, I helped Mum get the lunch ready and I noticed that Affie wasn't going to make any attempt at doing anything. She hung around talking to Peter for a bit but then he started to mow the lawn. I looked out of the kitchen window and saw Affie sitting on a deckchair with her Walkman and a magazine – one of mine, I noticed, that she had taken from my room without asking. Typical.

'I'm sure it will get easier,' Mum said, as if she had read my negative thoughts.

'You really think?'

'Well, you haven't been that friendly yourself, have you?' Mum commented.

'Give me a break, Mum! She's impossible!'

'She's finding it difficult, yes,' Mum said patiently. 'It's just as weird for Affie as it is for us. Please remember that.'

I couldn't think of anything to say that didn't make

me sound like a spoilt brat. A spoilt brat like Affie . . .

Peter was taking Affie home straight after lunch because she had suddenly announced that she simply had to get back so that she could go online with one of her friends. Peter didn't seem to want to argue with her. She went upstairs to get her things together and was gone for ages. I went up to the loo – and to make sure that she wasn't going to leave any of her junk behind in my room. When I went in to my room, there was Affie sitting on my bed. The camp-bed was a complete mess and Affie was just stuffing the last of her things in her bag, which I noticed was on my bed. The bed that I had made and she had messed up. It seemed like Affie was good at messing things up.

'Hope you haven't forgotten anything,' I said.

'I don't think any of this stuff is mine,' Affie said snootily as she looked around at my things – with a pitying look.

'I think this is,' I said, handing her the coffee mug that she had brought up with her and left on my desk. 'No!' I yelped in horror as I picked up the mug and saw that it had left one of those heat rings on the wood.

'Look what you did to my desk!' I screamed.

'Stressy!' Affie said dismissively. She just didn't care. She just didn't want to.

'It's ruined!' I yelled. 'You made a mark on my dad's desk!'

'Oh, please – give me a break!' Affie sighed and pushed past me to leave the room. 'It's just a mark.'

There was a thunder of footprints as Mum and Peter came upstairs to try to find out what the noise was all about.

'Something wrong?' Peter said anxiously, peering through the doorway.

'She's damaged my desk!' I spluttered. 'Look!'

'Where?' Mum said as Peter stood there looking as if he wished he was somewhere else. 'It's only a mark, Suzy. It's just an accident.'

I couldn't believe that Mum wasn't on my side! She knew it was Dad's desk! She knew it was special!

'She's ruined it!'

'Affie,' Peter said quietly, 'I think we should be going. And I think you should apologise to Suzy for putting that mug on her desk like that.'

'Sorry!' Affie said stroppily. 'OK – I fess up! I put a coffee mug on her precious desk! Der!'

She stomped down the stairs.

'I'll see you later,' Peter said to the pair of us and followed Affie out of the house.

And Affie didn't even say goodbye to Mum.

Chapter **Eleven**

Oh Dad!

Auntie Liz gave me this stuff today that you rub into wood. It's supposed to get rid of marks – marks like the one that Affie left on your desk. I rubbed it in really hard, like it said on the bottle and it's a bit better. Mum says that you can't see it at all. But I can. Cath says she can't see where it was. But I think she's lying, Dad. I know where it was.

Affie didn't give a toss about it either! She just didn't care. Nor did Mum, really! Why didn't she tell Affie off? She'd have told me off if I'd done something to Affie's stuff! It's just so not fair!

I'm going to put that stuff on your desk again tomorrow, Dad, to see if I can make it better. Promise.

LOL, Suze xxxx

* * *

Halfway through the next week, Peter told us he'd sold his flat. Clearly, Mum already knew about it, which sort of pissed me off and made me feel like piggy *out* of the middle.

'You'll never guess who rang me today,' he said, and without waiting for us to respond said, 'the estate agents! They've had an offer in for my flat and I've decided to accept it. So the good news is that we can put this house on the market now and get on with moving. Isn't that great?'

'That's a relief!' Mum said, looking at me anxiously. 'Isn't it, Suzy?'

'Yeah – sure,' I replied, sounding so like I really didn't believe it. Because I didn't.

'Tell you what, Suzy,' Mum went on, pretending not to notice. 'Why don't you and I go and see the estate agent tomorrow? Maybe we could even look at some new houses, too?'

'Great,' I mumbled. 'I can't wait.'

'Well, I think the idea of looking at new houses sounds quite fun!' Cath said as we sat on the grass in her garden the next day.

'Oh stop it!' I groaned. I was sitting in my running

gear because I'd stopped off there, mid-running session. 'You're beginning to sound like my mum! You'll be getting excited about bathroom tiles next.'

'Well, now you mention it . . .' Cath giggled. 'Oh, give your mum a break, Suze! You said yourself that your bedroom was small the other day. If you move, you'll be bound to get a bigger room. Lucky you!'

'My room was only small because dear Africa was in it! I've never had a problem with the size of my room before!' I protested.

'Exactly!' Cath said, sitting up and flicking her hair back. 'And Affie is going to come and stay loads of weekends from now on. Sometimes she'll even bring Indie with her!'

'Spare me!' I sighed, rolling on to my back and closing my eyes dramatically.

'So,' Cath went on, 'if Affie's going to come regularly, you don't want to have to put up with her trashing your room. So if you move to a new house, you'll have a new room and Affie will have her own room. So you won't have to share with her. Point taken?'

'OK, OK!'

There was silence for a while as Cath read her magazine and I contemplated what we'd just been talking about. It was true – if we moved then Affie wouldn't have to stay in my room. But if she had her own room in our new house, wouldn't that also make our house her house too? How unfair was that? Her house was with her mum, surely?

I thought about my room and how everything was exactly in the same place that it had always been. Except, of course, for Dad's desk, which was, if I was dead honest, filling the place up a bit. Maybe if I had a new room in some other house I would get a bigger room. And maybe I could make a kind of writing area. Somewhere to make the desk look really cool and where I could do my own writing. Just like Dad used to.

Maybe . . .

Much later that afternoon, I left Cath's and went the long way home so that I could have another run on the way back. Mum was still sitting at the kitchen table going through all the stuff she'd picked up at the estate agents about houses. She'd put them in three piles.

'What's this mean?' I asked, pouring myself a glass of milk and sitting down.

'The piles?' Mum said, looking up and smiling. 'This pile is the "yuck" pile. This one is the "possibly but not in an ideal location" pile. And these are the "great but at the top of our price range so we couldn't afford to do any work to it" one.'

'Oh,' I said and picked one up from the middle pile.

It was one of those houses that looks just like every other house in the terrace. Nothing ugly about it and nothing especially great about it either. I read through the stuff about how many bedrooms it had (enough to have a spare room that was presumably going to be Peter's study) and how big all the rooms were (which meant zilch to me). Then I saw where it was. Right on the other side of town. Miles from school and a million miles from Auntie Liz and Cath!

'No way!' I shrieked. 'I'm not going to live there! I'd have to get a bus to Cath's! And it would take me hours to get to school too!'

'I know,' Mum said. 'Don't worry – that's why it's in the middle pile. Suzy – we haven't even sold this house yet! We'll find somewhere that we'll all be happy with, I'm sure we will.'

Mum smiled at me and squeezed my hand. 'Fancy fish and chips for supper?'

'Yeah,' I agreed. It was months since I'd had fish and chips with Mum. We used to do it a lot when it was just her and me. We'd never done it with Peter. He was more of a restaurant than a fish-and-chips man and I wondered if he'd actually like them. I simply couldn't imagine him and Affie tucking in to cod and chips. I wondered if I'd ever have fish and chips alone with Mum again. And I felt a bit dumb to think like that. After all, it really was only fish and chips. How stupid could I be?

Later in the week, I went round to see Auntie Liz. She was up to her neck in decorating her bathroom when I arrived and said she was going to use me as an excuse to take a break.

'After all,' she said as she cut into one of her cakes, 'I've just finished the first coat and I can leave it to dry now while I have a nice chat with you.'

'Where's Ru?' I asked as we sat in her little conservatory room that was really just a greenhouse sort of thing at the back of the house.

'Oh he's gone over to Marco's house,' Auntie Liz said. 'It's quite nice to have got rid of him to be honest.'

'What?' I said, surprised.

'Well, all he and Marco get up to these days is kicking a football at each other and knocking the heads off my flowers. Or they sit in the living room and play that desperate war game on the console for hours.'

'Oh,' I said, realising that nothing much had changed then.

'So it's not me, then?'

'You? What do you mean sweetie?'

'I thought Ru had a problem with me,' I explained. 'I mean, he never seems to want to spend any time with me any more. Not like he used to.'

Auntie Liz smiled and shook her head. 'Of course it's not you, Suzy. It's Ru – and it's teenage boys. They go like that – well, most of them do. Surely you've noticed it at school with the other boys?'

'I don't really bother with the other boys in my class,' I said.

'There you are,' Auntie Liz replied. 'It's not just teenage boys; it's all of you!'

'I'm sorry,' I spluttered, feeling slightly offended that I was being associated with Ru's geeky behaviour.

'Can you honestly tell me that the girls in your class find all the boys as interesting as the boys in the older classes?'

'Well, no,' I replied. 'The boys in the other years are more . . . er, interesting. Cool.' I flushed with embarrassment as I thought about the fit boy in 11S.

'Huh. I remember when I was your age.' Auntie Liz laughed. 'I know it seems impossible that anyone can remember all that time ago. But I remember your dad. We'd got on quite well, really, for a brother and sister. Then suddenly – it was almost an overnight thing –

there were a couple of years when we all but hated each other. Your dad was two years older than me, but he behaved like he was younger than me.'

'I thought you'd got on well with Dad,' I said, feeling upset to hear her say something bad about Dad. I'd never heard her say anything like this about him before.

'Oh sweetie, we did,' she said, holding her hand over mine. 'By the time I was your age – maybe a bit older – we were really good mates again.'

'So why did it go wrong?'

'It didn't go wrong,' Auntie Liz explained. 'It just changed for a bit. You see, girls always seem to mature more quickly than boys. A couple of years ago you'd have been fine about playing your Game Boy with Ru, wouldn't you?'

I nodded.

'But when,' she continued, 'was the last time you even looked at your Game Boy?'

I thought. 'Can't remember.'

'Exactly! Give Ru a while to grow up and you'll be friends again. And he'll be wanting you to fix him up with a date with Cath.'

We laughed, and then I thought about him drooling all over Affie and Indie at the wedding and I shuddered. Yuck!

'So what else has been going on then?' Auntie Liz asked.

Then I told Auntie Liz all about the houses that Mum had been thinking about, and about Peter's flat being sold, and about how awful it had been when Affie had come to stay.

'Sounds like this new house is a good thing, then.'

'Except it could be miles away!' I whined. 'I want to still be here.'

'Well, your mum's not going to want to be too far from school, is she?' Auntie Liz pointed out. 'But you don't want to be right on top of your old house, do you?'

'Why not?'

'Because you'll need to get some distance from it,' Auntie Liz explained. 'Why on earth would you want to see someone painting your old bedroom or digging up the plants that you lovingly looked after? I certainly wouldn't want to see someone making my house look different from the way I'd left it.'

I could see what Auntie Liz meant.

'Look, I know it's a big change, Suzy, but try to think of it as an opportunity. You'll have a nicer room. More space so you're not all on top of each other. You might even end up closer to school! Or Cath. And you'll still be able to come and see me, won't you? I mean, it's not like your moving to the other end of the country.'

'Course I'll still come and see you – especially if you make more cakes like this one.'

We laughed together and then she said, 'Anyway – think of the fun you can have decorating your new room! If you play your cards right with your mum, she'll probably let you have any colour you want!'

I smiled at the thought. 'Maybe . . . '

'Tell you what,' Auntie Liz said. 'Why don't I buy you something for your new room, when you've got it? As a house-warming present for you?'

I swallowed my last piece of cake and hugged her. 'Oh thanks, Auntie Liz!'

Perhaps there were going to be some good things about this new house after all.

When I got home, Peter was sitting in the kitchen, surrounded by more bits of paper. He told me that Mum had gone round to see a friend.

'Not more house stuff!' I said, sitting down.

'What?' Peter looked up. 'Oh no – this is work. I came home early so that I could really concentrate on it – you know, without the phone ringing.'

It didn't look very easy for him from what I could see. One pile of work was on top of another. And

Mum's papers from the estate agent were all over the kitchen units. It was the usual chaos that Mum created when she was doing school stuff at home.

'I bet you must miss your flat,' I said, thinking of all that space and order that I remembered from when I had visited it.

Peter looked up at me and put down his pen. 'Not really Suzy, no,' he said, looking at me thoughtfully. 'It was a bit lonely, to be honest.'

'Lonely?'

'Yes – I much prefer it here, actually. I like living here with you and Donna. Even when the pair of you aren't here, this isn't a lonely house. It's a home. A cosy home.'

'Is it?' I said, surprised. I suppose I'd never really thought about it until Peter and all this moving stuff.

'Yes – full of things that have made you both happy. I'm looking forward to finding more space for them in our new house, though!' Peter laughed.

Now that really did surprise me!

'What – you mean we're going to take all this old stuff with us? I thought you'd want to have all your designer stuff in the new place.'

'Course we're going to take it with us to the new house,' Peter said. 'Especially the sofa.'

Actually, our sofa was a bit of a joke – even to Mum.

It was really old and tatty-looking with holes in the cover. But it was incredibly comfortable and Mum never moaned if you put your shoes on it.

'You're joking?' I said, looking at Peter.

'Not a bit, Suzy! Although, if you and Donna don't mind, I wondered if perhaps we could get it re-covered?'

I laughed and so did he.

'It might look better if it was,' I agreed.

'Good,' Peter said and smiled at me. 'Suzy – you know I'm really looking forward to choosing a new house with you. Our new house. Our home.'

I looked at him. Actually, I really believed him.

Chapter **Twelve**

I didn't realise until Affie came to stay with us every other weekend that it was possible to grow to dislike someone even more than you already did. But I did – with Affie. Not that Affie made any attempt to make friends with me either. In fact, she didn't try at anything. She wasn't interested in me. She wasn't even interested in trying to get to know Mum. All she did was moan about Indie being lucky enough to be in France and leave her things everywhere and never help with any of the cooking or even laying the table for a meal. Worse – Mum never ever told her off for it and instead even made excuses for her. How not fair is that? Peter sort of asked her to do things but he didn't seem to try very hard at it. It was almost as if he was scared of her. And you could tell that Affie really loved that.

As if it wasn't bad enough that we all had to put up with Affie's behaviour, Mum wouldn't let me go to

Cath's when it was one of Affie's weekends! Cath came round sometimes, and she even tried to talk to Affie, but it was like Affie was simply determined that she wouldn't be nice to her. In fact, she barely spoke to her either.

Still, I spent most of the remaining summer holiday with Cath. When her mum and dad announced that they were going on a camping holiday to Cornwall and would I like to go too, Mum said I could.

It was great. A whole week in a different place, sitting by the pool at the campsite and staying up late, giggling with Cath in our tent. The week seemed to flash by, and although I was pleased to see Mum and Peter when I got back, it would have been nice to have had another week there. Especially because no sooner had we got home, than it was time to get my school uniform out and go back to school. And the last weekend before I went back was extra cool because Affie didn't come for that one. Instead she and Peter drove Indie back to university. So not only did I not have to put up with Affie but I got Mum all to myself. It was weird, though, because the house seemed really empty without Peter there. I was kind of surprised how much I missed him.

It was obvious that Mum had spent all her time while I was away getting stuff ready for her classroom and her new Reception kids. There were piles of labels with elastic bands around them. And piles of name labels too. For once, though, everything wasn't all kind of jumbled up on the living room floor, in the hall and all over the kitchen. Sure, there was a lot of stuff, only when I got back, all the stuff was in piles, neat piles, on one side of the kitchen. There was also Mum's huge school bag, which was neatly stashed with other school things. I'd never seen Mum so organised before. No – that's wrong! Mum was organised. It's just that she's usually organised in a very jumbled-up sort of way.

'Hey, Mum – what's all this lot then?' I asked when we were having supper the first night I was back, just before Peter drove Indie back.

'Oh just all my school stuff, sweetie,' Mum explained. 'Actually, I'm going to take it all in tomorrow, you know, to get the classroom set up.'

'How come you're so, so . . . kind of sorted with it this term?' I asked.

'Thanks a bunch!' Mum smiled.

'Well, you know what I mean,' I said defensively.

Peter giggled. 'It is rather tidy, isn't it?'

'So what's changed?' I said.

'Well . . .' Mum looked at me and then at Peter and then back again. 'We've put the house on the market and the estate agent has already had a couple of lots of people book to come round.'

'What?' I put my fork down. 'You didn't tell me about that before I went on holiday.'

'But you know we're selling the house, darling.'

Peter said nothing and I just kind of stared for a bit feeling betrayed that Mum had gone and done something with Peter without telling me. I was thinking: of course I knew the house was being sold and I also knew there was nothing I could do about it. But I just wished they'd told me before I went away that people were coming round to gawp at my bedroom. And I knew that if I made a scene about it, it was just going to make me look stupid and like Affie. So I said nothing.

The silence was broken by the phone ringing. Mum answered it. 'Of course, darling. I'll just get him,' she said.

Darling? Who else did she call darling except for me? As soon as Peter took the phone from her, I knew – Affie! I felt stung. Surely I was Mum's only darling – except, of course, Peter? But that didn't really count.

Peter took the phone into the hallway while we carried on eating and Mum and I talked some more about my holiday. When he came back, he said, 'Well – it seems Affie's mother has to go on a course. Something to do with work, apparently. So Affie's going to have to come to stay with us for a couple of weeks while she's away.'

Peter sat down and smiled at Mum. It was one of those smiles that adults give other adults when they want them to give them a mental hug that says 'actually everything's going to be OK'. Mum smiled back at him. So it looked like it was sorted then. No choice. No one was going to ask me if it was OK, were they?

Affie was coming to stay for two whole weeks. Just great – NOT! Still, at least I had those couple of days alone with Mum, while Peter and Affie went off with Indie.

It's a disaster with a capital D, Dad!

Two whole weeks with that desperate girl in the house! I can't stand two days and one night with her without there being some kind of explosion. So how am I going to cope with her for fourteen days? Listening to Mum and Peter letting her get away with really bad stuff? And moaning about everything. Like it is SO NOT FAIR! No way am I going to live with her!

'I tell you, it's a nightmare, Cath!' I said during break at school on the first day of term. It was one of those fabulous September days when the sun shines and it's all warm and somehow seems even better than it was during the summer holiday. One of those days when you should really be allowed to be hanging out in the park instead of being locked up at school.

'Two whole weeks, eh?' Cath commiserated. '*Quel* nightmare! So what are you going to do?'

'What can I do?' I said. 'Precisely nothing. Affie's coming to stay and I don't exactly have any choice about it.'

'Hmm,' Cath mumbled. 'You've got to have a game plan. And then you've got to stick with it.'

'What game plan?'

'One so that you can manage to keep your cool with Affie.'

'Oh – like that's possible?' I spluttered dramatically.

'Your game plan should be to keep out of her way as much as possible,' Cath suggested.

'And how do I manage to do that in my own house? Shouldn't she be the one who keeps out of *my* hair?'

'Get yourself organised – hardly a problem for you, is it? Make sure you're out as much as possible. Running, round at mine and your Auntie Liz's. Do your homework in the library. If the pair of you avoid speaking to each other as much as possible, then you should get on loads better!'

We laughed. But I began to think that maybe Cath had a point . . .

Dad,
Well, I'm in Year Nine now. I can't believe that by the end of the school year, I'm going to have to have chosen all my exam subjects!

My new form teacher is called Mr Weston. He's OK I suppose – actually, that's not true. He's a bit geeky really. Some of the kids in the class have tried it on with him and, wow, has he got a temper!

We've got a new Spanish teacher too. Now she's cool: Senorita Esteria. She's fun, too. But everything else is the same old same old, really.

Mum's got her usual new school year buzz. She's been talking about all the new kids in her class. She's amazing you know. The kids come in crying for their mums on the first day but by the end of the week they're all having so much fun they don't want to go home. But – well, Dad, I suppose you are one of the only people who really knows how amazing Mum is.

Love, Suze xxxx

Chapter **Thirteen**

Affie arrived on a Sunday afternoon a week or so later. Instead of the usual backpack that she normally brought with her, she had a huge suitcase and a big school bag, too. On top of that was all her PE kit, including some weird stick thing that looked like a hockey stick with a net at the bottom of it.

'Hello, Affie – it's lovely to see you.' Mum smiled.

I noticed that Affie didn't when she said, 'Hi,' through pursed lips.

'Let's take your things upstairs, shall we?' Peter suggested.

'Then we could have some tea,' Mum said. 'I've made a cake – a chocolate one.'

'I'll come with you,' I said, bounding up the stairs behind Peter and Affie. I wasn't going to let her in my room without being there to see what damage she was doing.

Peter put her bags down in the corner, near Dad's desk.

'So where's my wardrobe, Dad?' Affie asked.

'Erm . . .' Peter didn't seem to know what to say.

I said nothing. Well, she wasn't going to have any of my wardrobe space – I mean, I hardly had room for my own clothes in there. There was definitely no room for hers, too.

'Everything all right?' Mum asked, standing on the landing. The room was too crowded for her to come in as well.

'I need a wardrobe to hang my clothes in,' Affie said impatiently.

Still I said nothing.

'Yes – of course,' Mum said, slightly flustered.

Mum sort of stepped forward and then back. Then she said, 'Suzy – why don't you empty one of your drawers so that Affie can use that?'

I glared at her. Like she thought I had enough space in my other drawers to cram the rest of the clothes in? She'd better not suggest I start emptying my wardrobe too, I thought. The problem was, as soon as I had these thoughts, I realised that if I did so much as to mutter any protest, I would immediately sound stupid and like I didn't want Affie in my room. And then everyone would think it was me who was being a pain. I couldn't win!

'OK,' I said frostily, and moved over to my chest of drawers. 'But there's absolutely no room in my wardrobe.'

I cleared things in my drawers in silence as Mum went and grabbed some coat hangers from her room.

'I wonder if perhaps you could use the hook behind the door in the study?' Mum suggested.

I turned round as I managed to make a satisfying slam when I shut my over-crammed drawer. Affie was looking in disgust at my mum's suggestion.

'Here – let me help you,' Mum suggested, opening Affie's suitcase.

'Thanks but I think I can manage on my own,' Affie said, really rudely.

'Why don't you two go and sort tea?' Peter said, panicking. 'I'll help Affie finish her unpacking.'

I was torn. I didn't want to be in that cramped room any longer. Especially not with her. But then I didn't want to leave her on her own in my room either. Of course, in the end, I went downstairs with Mum.

'Oh dear.' Mum sighed as she poured the boiling water into the teapot. 'That wasn't a very good start, was it?'

What could I say? She was so right. And it was all hers and Peter's fault.

★ ★ ★

'So did you burp and fart all night?' Cath giggled when I told her all about it during lunch the next day.

'Excuse me!' I said, pretending to look shocked. 'Oh I do so hope so!'

Cath laughed some more. 'But worse than that – did Affie?'

'You know, I think Affie is one of those people – those rare people – who doesn't know what a fart is. I'm quite sure that girls like Affie don't have bodily functions.'

We collapsed into more giggles as I tried to do an imitation of Affie looking her usual snooty self.

'So what are you going to do tonight?' Cath asked.

'Can I come back to yours?' I asked.

'Don't you need to go running?'

'Sure – but I thought I could come back to you after – you know, just for a bit?'

'No probs,' Cath said. 'If that's OK with your mum.'

Oh, Dad!
I came home from Auntie Liz's tonight and
Affie had come home first. And she'd spread
all her cack all over the place. All over my
bedroom. I don't know how she does it – I
mean, she's way worse than Mum is. She

puts her stuff on the floor, on the beds, on top of the chest of drawers – just everywhere. She is just so messy. And so stressy! If you ask her to move stuff it's like you've just told her she's the Weakest Link. Eee-ew! And we're not even halfway through her fortnight yet!

If it were me behaving like her dad, would you stand for it? Or would you be telling me off? Peter goes all silent on her and kind of stares at her. But he hardly ever seems to be about to tell her off. And the times when I think she's going to get it in the neck, he seems to have second thoughts and then doesn't say anything. Wimp!

Got to go, Dad, because I'm writing this while Affie's in the shower – I don't want to let her see me doing this. And I want to pretend to be asleep when she gets back. Otherwise I might have to talk to her. And that I just don't want to do!

Love, Suze

It was true. And now that Affie was in my room so much, and there were always people being shown around the house by the estate agent, I'd had to find a new hiding place for my letters box in Dad's desk, hidden deep under some school stuff.

'You should see the uniform she has to wear!' I groaned at Auntie Liz, one afternoon later in the week. I'd gone back to hers with Ru. Actually, let me rephrase that. I had followed Ru back from the bus stop because as soon as he had realised I was heading in his direction, he speeded up from his usual drippy crawl, almost like he was running away from me.

'What's so dreadful about her uniform?' Auntie Liz asked.

'It's just disgusting!' I explained. 'There's this awful stripy blazer. And she has to wear a tie. And she's *not* allowed to wear tights either – with this really scratchy-looking grey skirt.'

'Poor girl,' Auntie Liz commiserated.

I almost agreed with her and then stopped. I know if we'd been talking about anyone else, I would have said poor her. But I was talking about Affie and I couldn't let myself. I'd already told Auntie Liz about the mess Affie made, how she always looked as if she had a bad smell under her nose, and how she was always putting Mum down.

'She was telling us about some play she's in the other day,' I went on. 'She may go to some swanky private school, but they haven't got a proper stage or theatre to do the play on. All they've got are some wooden blocks that they move about to make a stage.'

I'd been really shocked when Affie had told us about it over supper one night. I mean, my school's got Arts Status and we had this fantastic new theatre built last year. It was opened at the end of the summer term by this really cool actor who's always on the telly and who lives nearby. They've even named it after him – The Leonard Theatre. It's a dead cool place and since it's been opened they've done loads of plays and shows there. Like I said, it's cool.

'I know Affie's a bit difficult,' Auntie Liz said. 'But I wonder if perhaps it's because she's finding it just as hard as you are? After all, she probably misses her mum, you know. And it must be really hard for her to know that her dad lives with you, don't you think?'

I looked at Auntie Liz and opened my mouth. But nothing came out. Was there no one in my family any more who was on my side?

The evening was even worse than the afternoon. Truly! I was helping Mum make the supper when Affie came in and just dumped her bag in the hall. She just about spluttered hello and then went into the living room to watch the telly. She didn't even attempt to offer to help. Then a few minutes later, Peter came in and tripped straight over Affie's bag. He went absolutely ape! I stayed in the kitchen, well out of the way, while Mum went out to see what all the fuss was about.

'Affie!' Peter yelled. I'd heard Peter cross before but I'd never heard him like that, and I'd never heard him lose it with his precious Affie before. He told her to move her stuff in no uncertain terms. Which she did. Sharpish. Even she seemed to realise how cross he was. Only I realised when I next went up to my room that she'd simply dumped her bag in the doorway of my bedroom for me to fall over when I went up there. That was it! As far as I was concerned, I'd put up with her crap for long enough. So I picked up her stupid school bag and emptied all of it over her camp-bed. Then I picked up all her other garbage – dirty clothes, books, shampoo, her hair irons – and shoved those on top of her bed for good measure.

Boy, did I feel good! At last I was getting my own back. Then, for the finishing touch, I grabbed some books from my bookshelf and made a long line of them leading from the doorway and to my bed. I'd made a dividing line so that there was my half of the room and another half that I was letting her borrow.

Then I went back downstairs and helped Peter lay the table. He was still really angry, I could tell. So I kept quiet and just did it in silence.

'Supper in ten minutes!' Mum called out to Affie, who was still watching the telly. Affie didn't reply, but I did hear her go upstairs. Then I heard her ranting and raving. Serve her right, I thought, feeling dead pleased with myself . . .

Chapter **Fourteen**

'**Suzy!** How could you?' Mum said, looking exasperated.

'Quite easily really,' I muttered, slightly under my breath – but not trying too hard to whisper. I just didn't care any more.

'That's enough!' Mum snapped.

'Donna,' Peter snapped and then stopped himself. He seemed to run out of the rest of his words.

Affie stood there, her eyes sparkling with fury. She was gaping at her dad.

'Dad, you just have to do something about this!' Affie demanded. 'She's ruined all my things!'

'Ruined? Me?' I spluttered. 'That's rich coming from you! You've invaded my room and trashed everything in there! It's *you* who's ruined everything around here!'

'Suzy! That's enough!' Mum yelled.

'Excuse me!' I exclaimed.

'So what are you going to do about it, Dad?' Affie demanded.

We were all upstairs, either crammed in my room or on the landing, gaping at Affie's little territory of mess.

Peter looked at Affie, then at me, then at Mum. He looked like a fish breathing under water. I felt quite sorry for him. Fancy having a daughter like Affie! I waited for him to tell her off.

'I think Suzy owes me an apology!' Affie said haughtily.

'You what?' I spat.

'Girls! That's enough!' Peter said, with such uncharacteristic sharpness that we all fell instantly silent.

Except for Mum who said, 'Really, Peter! I don't think there's any need to speak to them like that.'

So then Mum and Peter ranted at each other for a while! A real and proper row! I was quite shocked – I mean, I'd never seen them argue before. Ever. OK, they had minor disagreements and got tetchy – but I'd never seen a real bust-up before with raised voices. But I could see that Affie was loving it. Slowly, a sly little grin emitted from her face. She looked like someone who had run a race by tripping her main competitor up. She was such a bitch!

After a few minutes, Mum and Peter went silent. And

the silence was embarrassing. Suddenly, I felt like a fool. And looking at Affie, I wondered if she wasn't feeling pretty stupid too? But it didn't look like it to me.

'Donna – I am so sorry about this,' Peter said, putting his arm softly on her shoulder. Mum smiled at him. And then Peter turned to me and Affie and said, 'Girls, I think you both owe each other – and Donna – an apology. Then I think you should both clear up this mess and come down for supper.'

'What?' I spluttered and then fell silent again. Mum looked at me, clearly hurting at my behaviour, which made me feel really bad. But not only did I not want to say sorry, I didn't want to be the first one to say it. Affie stood and scowled, her lips pouting.

'Affie?' Peter said.

Affie said nothing and carried on staring at the floor.

'Affie – I am talking to you! Please at least give me the courtesy of a reply!'

Peter was looking seriously stressy. He clenched his teeth together as he spoke and he was all pink. If I'd been Affie it would have freaked me. But she just didn't seem to care. Either she was seriously cool or just stupid. Judging by Peter's flashing eyes, I'd say she was stupid.

'Affie! I will not say it again! Will you please apologise to Donna?'

More silence. More clenched teeth and eye flashing. But then she reluctantly said, 'Sorry,' as if the words would choke her.

'Sorry, Mum,' I said.

'Thank you,' Peter said. 'And now to each other.'

I felt like a baby! *Make up, make up – never do it again, or if you do you'll get the cane!* Honestly! But I could tell that we'd really upset Peter. In the end, we both kind of mumbled an apology. Peter told us to clear up the mess on our own and come downstairs to supper. Then he and Mum left us on our own.

'That girl just doesn't know when to give up, though!' I explained to Cath the next day on the journey to school. I'd made the story as dramatic as I possibly could – not that it really needed any embellishment because it really had been pretty desperate.

Actually, it had been awful. 'We're sitting there over supper, right, when Affie suddenly announces that she really needs to go into school a bit earlier today, so could her dad make sure he was ready quicker than he had been the rest of the week because he'd made her late!'

'You mean she hasn't been travelling in on the bus?' Cath asked.

'Not diddums!' I said. 'She gets her daddy to drive

her in every morning. Just like the baby she is.'

'No way?'

'Honest truth!' I said. 'So anyway, she's going on to Peter about it and he just loses it with her again. "I've got a meeting tomorrow morning at another office," he says. "You'll just have to get the bus like everyone else!" Way-hay! Re-sult!'

'So did she? Get the bus?' Cath asked.

'Course she did,' I said. 'Only she left ages before we did. Thank God! Otherwise we'd be with her now, wouldn't we?'

'Shame!' Cath grinned. 'I'd have really enjoyed the chance to chat with her.'

'Oh ha-ha!' I said sarcastically.

It was athletics club after school that day. So I travelled home on my own. Well, I say 'on my own'. What I really mean is that I didn't go home with Cath. There were some other kids from my school on the bus, including Ru and Marco, who were still trying to make out that they were in the athletics club. Only they didn't seem to take much notice of Mr Smythe, our coach. In fact, they spent most of their time pratting about and making Mr Smythe irritated. But, of course, Ru and Marco weren't interested in sitting on the bus with me. They were quite happy giggling about who knew what.

They got on the bus in front of me and went straight upstairs, where I had no doubt they were still monkeying about and would no doubt be told off by the driver, who could see their every move on his CCTV screen. I could see no point in following them, so I walked down the bus. That was when I came face to face with Affie who was sitting in the first double seat. She looked as shocked to see me as I was. We just blanked each other, saying nothing, and I went to sit right at the back of the bus. I felt a bit of a prat. The bus began to fill up with other kids as they slowly paid their fares and took up the other seats.

Pretty soon, Affie was surrounded, mostly by girls from Year Ten. From my observation place at the back, I could see them staring at her. Well, I mean, she really stuck out with her weird uniform. After the bus moved off, I heard one of the girls asking her where she went to school. Affie said nothing. The girl persisted and asked her again. In the end, I heard Affie replying.

'Dead posh!' the Year Nine said and everyone around her giggled hilariously.

I could see Affie staring out of the window. I bet she wished she was in Peter's car now, I thought, wondering if she usually had this hassle on the bus. She usually got a lift to school with Peter, but she either came home on the bus, or one of her mates' mums brought her back. I supposed, though, that if she'd been on the bus at this time on her own, most nights, there wouldn't be many kids from my school on it.

'So you got a boyfriend then at your school?' the Year Nine asked, leaning right into Affie's ear.

'No,' Affie said quietly.

'What's wrong with you then? None of them fancy you?'

All the girls around Affie laughed hysterically.

'There aren't any boys at my school,' Affie said, sounding sheepish.

'You mean like a convent then?'

And they all giggled again. It looked like someone else was at least giving Affie a dose of her own medicine. But for some reason it was making me feel uncomfortable.

Chapter **Fifteen**

The Year Ten girl didn't seem to want to give up on Affie. Perhaps it was because every time she taunted her, all the other girls she was with rewarded her with adoring laughter. The girl was loving it and it didn't really surprise me because she had a bit of a reputation for being a bully in school. Well, she's often being sent to the head anyway.

But when the girl leaned right over Affie and demanded her tie, even I began to sense that the situation was getting a bit strong. I was feeling anxious – so I reckoned that Affie was definitely feeling like she wanted to escape. I sat listening, feeling pathetic at the back from the comfort of my seat. Still the taunting carried on. The girl was tugging at Affie's tie, and I heard Affie asking her to leave it alone. Her voice sounded squeaky. And scared. Which made the girls around her worse.

We were nearly at our bus stop but I wasn't sure how much more of the girl Affie could take. The bus was beginning to slow down for the next stop. I looked over and saw the Year Ten girl trying to look inside Affie's bag. It was getting too much, and I didn't see why even Affie should have to put up with her any longer. Without thinking, I quickly stood up and rushed to the front of the bus, just as it was coming to a halt.

'Hey – I didn't see you there!' I said, leaning over Year Ten girl and grabbing Affie. 'Come on or we'll miss our stop. Bye!' I waved at the others as if nothing had ever been wrong. They looked surprised and said nothing. The ringleader sat there with her mouth open – like a baby who'd had her dummy pulled out of her mouth. Whatever, it had made her speechless.

Affie looked a bit stunned at first, but then she just fell in with me and stood up. She was holding her bag as if her life depended on it. When the driver opened the doors, we hopped down, me still holding Affie's arm like she was my best mate. We just walked, quickly, towards home. It was such good acting I should have been auditioning for a part in the next school production. I could tell from the way she sighed that Affie was as relieved as I was when the bus doors closed behind us and it pulled away. As it drove off in front of us, I let go of Affie, who immediately pulled herself away from me. The pair of us slowed our pace in silence.

Eventually I said, 'You OK?'

Affie's face was pale and tight. She didn't look OK.

'I'm fine. Er, thanks,' she said, obviously lying.

'No worries,' I said, continuing the pretence. 'Just a shame we've got to walk an extra bus stop home, eh?' I tried to laugh but it didn't really work.

We carried on walking in an awkward silence for a bit and then I said, 'Don't take it personally. You know, those girls on the bus, they're like it with loads of people. They're always bullying people at school and getting in trouble.'

Affie looked at me as we walked. Then she said, 'Thanks for your concern, Suzy, but actually, I was fine. There really was no need for you to worry about me. I can handle girls like that.'

You could have fooled me, I thought. But I said nothing. Affie really pissed me off! Even after a thing like that she couldn't lighten up at all. We walked in an awkward silence the rest of the way home.

Hi, Dad,
Sorry – I haven't been able to write for a few days. It's so difficult trying to find a

moment with Affie around. I'm writing this now instead of doing my homework. Well, Mum thinks I'm doing my maths, but I've got my notepaper stuck between the pages. Mum hasn't noticed how much writing I'm doing because she's making a patchwork elephant. It's something for the kids in her class.

I can't wait for Affie to go home, Dad! There's another week to go still. A whole long week. She's so boring. And so stressy! She's changed the whole atmosphere in the house – no one seems to be able to laugh any more. Not me and Mum. Nor Peter. And I don't think Affie has ever laughed in her life!

Worse. Ru keeps coming round! Normally, I'd be pleased that he wants to see me. Only he doesn't want to see me – he wants to drool around Affie! And so does Marco. They just stand in the room near her and hardly say anything. Except you can almost see the dribble coming out of their mouths as they swoon. They obviously fancy the pants off her. But even

Affie's not interested in drongos like them.
Not that those saddos seem to realise.

I tried to help Affie out with some bullies
today but afterwards she acted as if I'd done
her a bad turn. I wish I'd left her to get on
with it now. Cow!

LOL, Suze xxxxxxx

We had pizza for supper that night and Mum asked Affie and me if we would help her with the toppings. Mum buys these plain bases in the supermarket and then we always have loads of fun doing our own toppings. We've done some really weird and wacky ones in the past.

As Mum and I got stuck in, Affie kind of looked at us. Like she didn't know if she was allowed to join in.

'Come on, Affie – you can use anything you like that's in the fridge,' Mum said. 'Even the pickle if you like!'

'Oh yuck, Mum!' I giggled, remembering the time when Ru had made a pickle and baked bean pizza. It must have tasted as revolting as it had looked.

'OK,' Affie said stiffly, looking at what I was doing for guidance.

'Do you do much cooking at home?' Mum asked her.

'No,' Affie replied. 'I mean, Mum doesn't have time to cook. She's always late back from work. Sometimes she doesn't get home until I've already gone to bed.'

'So you spend the evening alone?' I asked, incredulous.

'Yes – no,' Affie said. 'I mean, if my mum isn't coming back until really late, our cleaning lady comes and sits with me for a bit. But it's stupid, really, because I don't actually need a babysitter any more.'

Cleaning lady, eh? I thought. Perhaps that explains why Affie doesn't have a clue about keeping the place tidy because she simply never has to. Typical – she was waited on hand and foot.

'So does your mum cook at the weekends then and pop things in the freezer?' Mum asked.

'Oh, Mum doesn't like cooking,' Affie said. She sounded a bit sad. 'Mum says her talents lie elsewhere. She does a mega shop at the supermarket on Sunday morning. There's always loads of stuff in the fridge. Or we have takeaways. It's cool.'

She didn't sound like she thought it was cool, though. But as she got into her pizza toppings, it looked as if Affie was actually enjoying it. She certainly seemed to like it when we got to eat them a bit later on. By then, Peter had got home and he was definitely enjoying the pizza that Mum had asked Affie to make for him.

As we ate, we talked about what we'd all done that day. Mum told us some story about how she'd discovered an outbreak of nits in her class. Affie looked horrified but even she started to smile when Peter started itching. He said it was just the thought of the kids' nits that made him itch! Peter told some story about a man with really terrible BO that he'd had to have a meeting with. And Affie and I just told everyone what we'd been doing at school. Although Affie had to be really pushed into talking by Peter, I noticed. She didn't really want to tell anyone anything, you could tell. Neither of us mentioned what had happened on the bus.

As a special treat, Mum said we could have ice cream for pudding. We were busy tucking in when Affie said, 'Dad – could I have a lift home from school tomorrow?'

Peter looked at her and said, 'Sorry darling, I'm in court all day tomorrow with a client and I've no idea when it will end. You can catch the bus, can't you?'

Affie looked at him blankly. 'Sure – course I can.'

She didn't eat any more ice cream after that.

Chapter **Sixteen**

'**So** let me get this right,' Cath said as we ate our lunch the next day. 'You – that's you, Suzy – are feeling sorry for Affie?'

'Well, not sorry exactly – just . . . it's just that from what she said last night, I don't think that living in her house sounds like it's much fun.'

'Like I said, then. You feel sorry for her.'

'God, you can be just so irritating some times.' I laughed.

'Doesn't sound like her mum's got much time to be with her,' Cath said. 'And with Indie away at university it's not really surprising that she wants to be with Peter so much, is it?'

I hadn't thought about it like that before. Maybe Cath was right. Perhaps it was because she spent so much time on her own after school that Affie was always ringing her dad and getting him to come to pick her up.

'Well, I think it's sweet,' Cath said.

'What's sweet?'

'The way you are so concerned about your sister,' Cath said, grinning.

'Get lost! She's not my sister!' I spluttered.

'She's your stepsister, isn't she? I rest my case!'

I spent the rest of the day thinking about Affie when I should have been concentrating on other things. Like school work – at least occasionally. It was just so irritating! Why was I wasting my time on her? But what I'd been talking about with Cath did make me wonder if Affie was actually just lonely. After all, she never seemed to go back with any friends after school. Nor did she spend much time on her mobile.

Because it was Friday and I wanted to get my homework out of the way, I didn't go to Auntie Liz after school or for a run. Instead, I went home so that I could have some peace and quiet before the house filled up for the weekend. So I was surprised to hear the telly when I walked into the hall. I knew there was no way that Mum would already be home from school. Maybe it was Peter, back early from his day in court?

But in the living room I found Affie. She wasn't in her school uniform and she was watching *The Chart* on digital. It was at least an hour before she'd been back any other night that week, and I wondered how come she was there.

'Hi,' I said, slumping down on the sofa.

'Hi,' she replied, not taking her eyes off the telly.

'Didn't you have to go to school this afternoon?'

'Er, no.'

Affie was proving to be as friendly as usual, and she didn't take her eyes off the screen. But it seemed weird to me because she hadn't mentioned it yesterday. And hadn't she asked Peter to bring her home? She certainly hadn't told him that she was going to be early.

'You OK, Affie?' I asked.

'Course I am,' she snapped. 'Why wouldn't I be?'

'Sorry – I just thought maybe you'd come home early because you were ill or something.'

'I said I'm fine, didn't I?'

'Sor-ree.'

It was after that that Affie just exploded. 'What is it with you and your mum? All you ever do is ask if everything is OK – constantly wanting to know what I'm up to and when. What's it got to do with you lot?'

'Since when was it a crime to be interested in people?' I spluttered.

'Nosy, more like!' Affie spat.

'Nosy?' I protested. 'What makes you think we're interested in you and your stuck-up life? It's obvious that you think we're not good enough for you. But your mum obviously thinks we're good enough for you to come and stay with us while she goes away on her holiday.'

I could feel my ears going red with anger. And embarrassment. Because I knew what I'd just said was a bit unkind. I knew that her mum was on a course to do with work, not a holiday.

'Don't you dare talk about my mother!' Affie continued. 'My mum works really hard, you know.'

'Yeah – so hard that you never see her!'

You could almost see smoke coming out of Affie's ears as soon as I said it.

'I do too! I live with her, don't I? We can't all be like you and have a mum and a dad with us every night, you know.'

'My father is dead!' I pointed out.

Affie caught her breath for a second. 'Well, your own dad may be dead, but you get more time with my dad than I do, don't you?'

I looked at her, not sure what to say. After all, it was true – I did live with her dad. Which must have been irritating to Affie.

'Well, at least you get to see your dad some of the time,' I said. 'I never ever get to see mine any more, do I?' There was a nasty taste in my mouth but I carried on. 'And you don't have to share your mum either, do you? Not like I do – calling you darling all the time and putting up with your bad moods and mess! You get away with murder in this house, you do!'

Affie looked at me aghast. Clearly what I'd said was reaching her somehow. Eventually she said, 'I'm sorry. I didn't realise that you were so angry about me coming here.'

'Angry?' I asked both her and myself aloud. Was I angry? Suddenly it seemed ridiculous to be angry with someone who had no choice about things. Just like I had no choice. I knew, really, that it wasn't Affie's fault that she was here. Just circumstances. 'I'm not angry,' I said finally. 'I just hadn't realised quite how much you resented me living here with your dad.'

Affie said nothing and just stared at the telly. It was obvious, though, that she wasn't watching it. Eventually, she spoke quietly. 'It's not true. I don't get away with murder. All I ever get these days is a hard time. Like I'm an inconvenience and in everyone's way – including my dad's.'

'You're pissed off with me, aren't you?' I urged.

Still Affie said nothing.

'Thought so,' I said and also sat in silence for a while. Then I said, 'You know, you're lucky to have a sister, Affie. All I've got is Ru – and all he wants to do these days is fart and giggle with his mate Marco.'

Despite herself, Affie laughed. 'He's a bit of a geek, isn't he?'

We laughed together and I felt some of the tension ease.

'It's not always brilliant to have a sister, though,' Affie said.

'What do you mean?' I asked.

'We argue a lot – me and Indie,' Affie explained. 'And she's just so kind of perfect, you know? She did brilliantly at school and never got into trouble. She's always looking great too. Do you know, I don't think she's ever had a spot in her life?'

We giggled some more.

'I'd never really thought a sister being a pain,' I admitted. 'I've just always wished I'd had one.'

'Well, sisters have their moments, believe me.'

'Listen,' I said a few minutes later. 'Do you fancy some tea? And shall we see if there is any cake left?'

'OK,' Affie said. And she followed me into the kitchen.

Hey, Dad!
I know you used to fight with Auntie Liz
when you were a kid but were you honestly

as irritating as Ru is, I wonder?

Dad – you know all those things I've
been telling you about Affie? Well, I had a
talk with her today – actually it was more
of an argument. It's weird you know, it's the
first time we've ever really talked to each
other. I kind of got to know more about
her. Found out that she's a bit lonely, I
think. And that maybe things in her house
aren't as cool as she's tried to make out.

You know, even though she's still got her
dad, I think she misses him just like I miss
you. No wonder she hates me! I think she
thinks that I've won her dad and she's the
one who's lost. Poor old Affie.

But listen to me, Dad! Here's me feeling
sorry for someone who's made my life dead
miserable over the last week. Maybe she's
getting to me more than I thought.

It's the weekend tomorrow. We're going
with Mum and Peter to look at some houses
while the estate agent shows people round
here. Promise I'll only like the houses that I
think you would have wanted to live in.

Kisses, Suze xxxxxxxxxxxx

Chapter **Seventeen**

In fact, Mum and Peter had looked at quite a lot of houses already. I'd gone to see a couple of them too but I'd got bored with the whole thing after that. Sniffing around other people's kitchens isn't nearly as interesting as it always looks on those decorating programmes on the telly. The houses they were taking us to see were the ones they thought were worth a second look. You see, there was this couple who the estate agent was convinced was going to make an offer on our house. So it seemed like the pressure was on for us to find somewhere to buy after all these weeks of faffing around and tidying up. To be honest, I was quite glad that after all the talking – and all the room sharing – something finally seemed like it was going to happen.

The first house we looked at was just disgusting! Every room had this truly revolting wallpaper and the loo downstairs was a dark brown colour. Peter said that it had been all the rage way back in the 1970s when he was a teenager to have rooms that colour. Gross. Affie said the kitchen (dark brown, once-shiny units, and orange and fudgy-coloured wall tiles) looked like a migraine had hit it. She was right! But Mum was seriously worrying because she kept on saying how light the house was and how much potential it had. Surely she had to be mad to think we should move to it?

And so the day went on with us looking at houses and being followed around by estate agents and the house owners who seemed to be desperate to get us to buy their house. When the people who owned the houses were there too, it was hard because you couldn't say out loud what you were thinking in your head about how dirty they were or what pitiful taste they had in decoration. Mum and Peter seemed to think that every house was fantastic from what they said, but I began to think that they must be headcases. Or just plain antique saddos.

But then, late in the afternoon, after I thought we had seen the last grotty house, Peter got a call on his mobile from one of the estate agents. She'd just had someone pull out on a house and thought we might like to see it. It was empty because the people had moved and she could meet us there in ten.

'Dad!' Affie wailed. 'I thought you said we could go home and have something to eat!'

'Yes!' I said, for once agreeing with her in public.

Mum and Peter looked at each other and smirked.

'I know,' Peter said. 'But this house is in exactly the right place. And if it's as good as it sounds, we could be the first people to see it. I promise we won't be long.'

The estate agent was already waiting for us when we got there and the really good news was that the house was in the road around the corner from Cath's.

'Glad you could make it,' the estate agent said, smiling. 'Feel free to roam wherever you want to – you won't disturb anyone. And there's no brown loos either, I promise!' She smiled at us as she unlocked the house and we followed her in.

'Shall we go upstairs?' I said to Affie. 'Check out the bathroom properly?'

'OK,' she agreed and lead the way up the stairs.

The woman was right – everything was white. There was even a separate shower in there. Not bad. Affie and I had a wander. All the bedrooms were about the same size – and all of them were way bigger than my bedroom at home.

'This place is big,' said Affie, as I followed her into one of the bedrooms. 'This is the fourth bedroom! And what's behind this door?'

'Must be a cupboard,' I suggested.

Only it wasn't – it was another bathroom! Smaller than the first one we'd seen but exclusive to this one bedroom. 'Cool,' I said.

Mum and Peter followed us into the room. 'Any good?' Mum asked.

'This one's got four bedrooms!' Affie said. 'It's big.'

'Well – you need your own bedroom,' Mum pointed out.

'Who? Me?' Affie said, sounding surprised. 'Here?'

'Of course, darling,' Peter said, going up to her and putting his arm around her. 'And, of course, we need a room for Indie to stay in when she comes, too.'

'I didn't realise,' Affie said and she gave a relieved smile.

You could tell that she was gobsmacked that our new home was for her as well. I was just pleased that I was no longer going to have to share with her once we moved and surprised that Affie hadn't realised before.

'What's this?' Mum said, going in to the small bathroom. 'Hey! It's got an *en suite*!'

'Excellent!' Peter said, looking in there with her. 'That means the girls could have the bigger bathroom and I won't have to hang around for hours any more waiting for my daughters to be finished.'

I'd never heard Peter call me his daughter before and it sounded weird. I could see Affie flinch a bit and I felt embarrassed that he had. Although if I'm honest, I didn't really mind that he'd said it. It didn't really seem to be bothering me that much.

'Come on,' I said to Affie and we went downstairs to look around there while Peter and Mum carried on discovering the upstairs.

It wasn't bad. There was a big living room and the kitchen was loads bigger than the one in our old house with tons more room for a table and stuff. And there were two big french doors going out into the garden.

'Like it?' the estate agent asked, as we peered outside.

'It's OK,' Affie said, sounding like she meant it.

'Is that a tree house?' I asked, pointing to something I could see at the end of the garden.

'Yes,' the woman said. 'Only I expect you two wouldn't be interested in that.'

Hmm, I thought. It just might be somewhere to hide from Affie if she got painful like she'd been earlier in the week . . .

By the end of the weekend, all of us had decided that the last house was the one – the only one – that we all liked. I wanted to go back and see it so that I could bags the best of the bedrooms before Affie got a chance. Not that I said that of course. Mum was in a mope, though, because she'd decided that we *had* to have *that* house and she was worried that we wouldn't get it because our house hadn't been sold and this house that we wanted cost loads more money than they'd planned.

Hey, Dad!
Do you hate me now? Are you dead cross
with me? I'm worried that you might
because I've decided that I do want to move
now. I really like that house we saw! I'd have
a much bigger bedroom. I want the one on
the furthest end of the landing because it's
way away from the room that Peter and
Mum will have so I'll be able to watch telly
in bed and they won't be able to hear it! I
know I haven't got a telly yet, Dad, but if I
save up all my birthday and Christmas
money and some pocket money, I ought to
be able to buy one. And if I get it for myself,
then Mum won't be able to moan about it!
    I'm really going to miss this house –
honest. But the new one is only around the

corner, really. And it's nearer to Cath! And it's not that far from Auntie Liz, either. But the best thing is that I'll have a corner where I can put your desk and your stuff. A proper sort of study place where I can do my writing. Because I want to be a writer, just like you.

Really love you, Dad! Always.

Suzy xxxxxxxxx

On Monday afternoon there was some good news on the house front. The couple who liked our house had made an offer and Mum snapped it up. But it didn't solve everything because Peter and Mum then got super stressy about buying the other house. For a whole week, all they both talked about was mortgages and offers. It was dead boring. All I wanted to do now was move and have a bigger bedroom.

Boy, was it tense in our house! Every time more information was sent about other houses, Mum read them and made tutting noises about how they weren't as nice as 'the' house. And Peter kept saying that he was still in negotiation with the agent over 'the' house.

The following weekend, though, Peter came home from work with a grin on his face. It was sorted:

because our buyers wanted to move quickly, the agent had persuaded the other people to go with us buying their house because we could move in soon. There was a whole load of yawn-making stuff about the money being tied up in an empty house and them having moved to Wales because of work. Whatever, somehow or other, Peter and Mum had sorted the money problem – something to do with Peter getting a promotion. So it was double grins all round really. At last – and at one time I never thought I'd say it – we were moving!

Chapter **Eighteen**

'**So** let me get this straight,' Cath said to me some months later as she lay on the bed in my new bedroom. 'You're going to paint this wall bright pink and the other walls are going to be white?'

'Don't you think that will look cool?' I spluttered, suddenly beginning to doubt the major decision that had taken me yonks of agonising to come to.

Cath looked at me and then giggled. 'Joke!'

I was relieved, because I hadn't actually ever chosen the colour scheme in my bedroom. In my old house, I'd just stuck with how it had been (boring white all over, actually) for always. After my dad had died, I hadn't really wanted to change it. Sure, I changed some of the posters and stuff like that. But otherwise it was just the same. So this new bedroom, in this new house, was a major move for me.

'Can I see Affie's room?' Cath asked.

I wasn't sure. It seemed a bit kind of rude to go in Affie's room when she wasn't there, really. 'Dunno,' I said.

'Oh come on,' Cath nagged, getting up and going in there anyway.

Affie's room was the one nearest the bathroom. She reckoned it meant she had the advantage because it was almost like having her own bathroom. I just knew that I had the bathroom to myself most of the time, so I didn't care.

'Is it dead stylish?' Cath wanted to know as she barged in. In fact, there wasn't much in the room and it was pretty bare. 'Oh.'

'Well, she hasn't really had much time to do stuff to it, has she?' I said, finding myself defending her.

'What colour's she going to paint it?'

'She talked about some kind of blue,' I explained. 'But I don't think she's made up her mind. But I do know it's loads easier now that she's got her own room to dump all her kit in instead of spreading it out all over mine. Indie will be able to sleep in the other room. Mum's got ideas about painting it a sort of ivory colour. Something she saw on a makeover show on the telly.'

'Cool. So do you like it here?' Cath asked me, looking out of the window into the garden.

I thought for a bit then said, 'Well, it's different from the old house . . . but I do like all the space. It's not so cramped with all Mum's junk and Peter's stuff.'

'And having a bedroom that's about three times the size can't be so bad either!' Cath said, sounding envious.

'That's not so bad either.' I laughed.

Hi, Dad,

It seems a bit weird to say this but I think you'd like it in this house. It's sort of the same shape as our old one but just kind of bigger in every direction. So it reminds me of our house only it's different. And your desk is brill in my room! I've put it under the window – I think you'd have chosen that place, too. That way you can see out of the window when you write.

There's this old tree house in the garden – it's right at the end. It was probably made for some kids who used to live here but it's really cool. Peter was going to pull it down but I asked him not to. It's a good thinking place, Dad, when the weather's warm. Affie and I have put in some cushions and things to sit on – it's a bit like having an extra bedroom. Cath spends time there with me too when she comes round.

We got the RE-COVERED sofa cover back today! We've had it covered in denim and it looks dead cool! It was Peter's idea. When he first suggested it, I thought he was nuts. But he said that denim would go soft and wear in like a pair of old jeans so that the sofa would look different but still be like an old friend! He's right! I can't believe that I live in a house with a trendy sofa – it's like one of those things you see in a magazine!

Being here when Affie is here isn't nearly so difficult now that she's got her own room either. She seems happier about it too. But she still rings Peter up all the time, asking him to take her places. But I don't think she does it just because she's jealous of him being here. I think it's also because she really hasn't got someone to collect her sometimes, with her mum working such long hours. Mum works hard, I know, but at least she can bring her stuff home from the classroom and do it here.

We don't see so much of Indie, though. She rings sometimes – she's always friendly if I answer the phone. But she hardly ever comes home from university. I bet she's got loads of boys who fancy her because she's really cool and beautiful. Mum gave me a photo of you that she had in the photo album. We'd been looking at in when we were unpacking here. It's really weird how moving house makes you look at all your things as if they are new and that you've never really seen them before! But we were unpacking the albums – all the stuff that we used to keep in that wooden box thing in the hall of our old house – and we stopped to look at the photos. It was good, looking at you, Dad. And there was this photo of you and Mum that Mum says Auntie Liz took when you two first met. It's a bit fuzzy and you both look dead weird in your gross clothes! But you look really happy too. Mum said it was wasted in the album so I've put it in a frame and it's on my desk – your desk – now.

Still love you loads, Dad.

Suze xxxxxxxxx

* * *

'Well, my goodness!' Auntie Liz said one afternoon. She'd met me at the bus stop and had come round to the new house for a cup of tea. It wasn't the first time that she'd been to see us of course – she'd been round for a meal with Uncle Joe and Ru one Saturday. It was OK but Ru was just boring. He kept asking why Affie wasn't there (he still dribbled when he said her name) but other than that all he had to say was the odd grunt. I suppose it was better than him giggling or farting. But not much. I'd wondered if it was ever going to be the same again with Ru, like Auntie Liz said – like it used to be when the pair of us were friends - but at the moment, it didn't seem likely.

'This is really pink!' Auntie Liz said as she saw the results of a weekend's painting party.

'Affie and Cath helped me,' I explained.

'Really?' Auntie Liz smiled. 'That sounds like a good idea – spreading the load so that you don't have to do it all on your own.'

'Well, I said I'd help Affie next time she comes for the weekend,' I said. 'She's picked this really gorgeous blue – it's kind of iridescent and shimmers in the light.'

'I'm glad you're getting on with her,' Auntie Liz said, sitting down at Dad's desk.

I cringed when she said it. Why did they all have to

make such a big deal about Affie and me 'getting on' with each other? I mean, yes, it was OK most of the time with Affie. But it wasn't like she was instantly my best friend or anything. I still found the way she left the bathroom dripping in her wet towels the most disgusting thing in the world (after Ru and Marco being in the same place at the same time, that is – which was a truly excruciating experience). And she was still rude to Mum sometimes (although not so often, granted) and she always, *always* managed to ring Peter during meal times (it was almost a joke in our house that when the phone rang as we sat down, it would be Affie). But, we didn't have great rows like we had in the old house. Smaller rows sometimes, but not such big ones. And painting the room with Affie and Cath had been quite fun, I suppose.

'It's OK,' I said to Auntie Liz. 'I don't think she minds me being with Peter quite so much any more. Fancy some tea?'

I wanted to change the subject to be honest, and thankfully, Auntie Liz followed me down to the kitchen where life couldn't be quite so personal. I hoped.

'So how's Ru these days?' I asked.

How weird was that? Like I didn't go to the same school as Ru every single day of the week and here I was asking about him as if I never saw him? But I didn't see nearly so much of him any more because if he ever saw me in the corridor at school he just acted like he didn't know who I was and giggled with Marco. Der brain!

'Ru's OK,' Auntie Liz said. 'He still spends lots of time playing those games with Marco – you know, the ones on the telly console?'

I nodded.

'But I don't think he spends nearly as much time doing his running – does he?' Auntie Liz asked.

'He still comes to the athletics club at school,' I said. 'But I don't think he's that bothered about it any more.'

What I didn't tell Auntie Liz was that Ru had been told that if he didn't stop mucking about so much he would be kicked out of the athletics' club. Ru may have been dead irritating, but I didn't want to snitch on him. But fortunately, I heard a key in the door.

'That's Mum!' I said, jumping up and switching the kettle back on. 'Fancy a top up?'

I was sitting with Peter and Mum at the kitchen table that night, halfway through our supper when the phone rang.

'I'll go,' Peter said, not having to even mention Affie's name.

I started chatting to Mum about the new kitchen units that she and Peter were thinking of putting in (how sad am I that kitchen units are now vaguely – OK 'quite' – interesting to me these days?), but then Peter came back with the phone and said, 'Suzy, it's for you.'

He handed the phone to me and I looked at him blankly. Any mates of mine would either text me or call me on my mobile. No one rang me on the real phone any more.

'It's Affie,' Peter explained. 'She wants a word.'

Affie was calling me? This was a first. I took the phone from Peter.

'Hello?'

'Suzy? It's Affie. Listen, I was wondering,' Affie's voice was fast and animated. You could tell she was excited about something. 'Mum's going to take me shopping on Saturday for some stuff for my new bedroom – the one at yours – and I wondered if you'd like to come and help me choose?'

I was gobsmacked. This was not something I was expecting. 'Um.'

But before I could say any more, Affie carried on, 'I asked Mum and she said it was OK if it's OK with your mum. She thought we could go to Harvey Nichols and she's going to take us out to lunch after.

This Saturday. You up for it?'

Harvey Nichols? Lunch in some swanky part of London? With Affie? With *Affie's mum*? I really didn't know. I mean, Harvey Nichols was a big deal. And so was going there with Affie. And I wasn't sure about it.

'Suzy? You still there? You can come, can't you?'

'Um,' I mumbled. 'Let me ask Mum. Hang on.'

I explained to Mum who looked surprised and glanced at Peter before saying, 'Of course that would be OK Suzy. How kind.'

'Sure, Affie,' I said, beginning to realise that a day in London, shopping, would be quite cool. And as Affie had done it loads of times, she'd presumably know all the places to go. 'So what time?'

Dear Dad,
Is life all about things happening that you
don't expect? I am going to spend Saturday
with Affie and her mum shopping! It should
be cool – but how weird is it that a few
months ago I wouldn't have wanted to do
that at all? Not that I would have been
invited, I don't think! I wonder what Affie's
mum is like? Affie told me once that she
was called Harriet. I bet she looks like Indie

and wears these dead trendy clothes and doesn't look anything like a mum! Well, not like Mum, anyway.

Sometimes, I lie in bed at night, wondering what I'm going to be doing in a year's time. Or ten years' time – or even twenty years' time. Will I be married and have kids? Will I be living on my own with some swanky sports car? Or will I have won the London Marathon? I kind of want to know. But I kind of don't want to know either! I want it all to be a surprise – but I don't want any more surprises like losing you, Dad. Never ever.

I'm sorry I don't write to you so often any more. It's not that I don't think of you just as much – I do, I think of you all the time! But I don't seem to have so much time to write. There's loads of new stuff going on since we moved here. Most of it's good too. Really good.

I love you, Dad. Loads. And I'll write again as soon as I can.

Suze xxxxxxxxxx

If you would like more information about
books available from Piccadilly Press and how
to order them, please contact us at:

Piccadilly Press Ltd.
5 Castle Road
London
NW1 8PR

Tel: 020 7267 4492
Fax: 020 7267 4493

Feel free to visit our website at
www.piccadillypress.co.uk